A Cr

By

James Mullaney

James Mullaney

Cover art © 2013 Micah Birchfield All Rights Reserved

Micah's Web Site:gentlemanbeggar.wordpress.com

Editing and Formatting

Donna Courtois and Dale Barkman sunnyjoe@att.net

To my real-life Albion friends who get the joke: please explain it to the mob with the pitchforks and torches in my front yard. They're stomping on my geraniums.

Note from Jim:

If you enjoyed this book, please take a moment to post a positive review at Amazon, and spread the news at your personal web site, Facebook page, etc. I don't know if these simple kindnesses will get you into Heaven, but they might help to keep the author out of the unemployment line. -- Jim Mullaney

James Mullaney

Chapter 1

The old steam-fed radiator in the cobwebbed corner clanked and howled like a cell block packed with inmates in full protest mode, banging their battered tin cups off the iron bars and groaning about the lousy prison grub.

Lucky for me the hangover I was nursing wasn't the usual Bikini Atoll H-bomb testing kind that was my Monday morning garden variety or I'd've ripped the clattering noisemaker from the warped spot on the damp wood floor where it had been bleeding moldy black stains for the past hundred years and given it the old heave-ho out onto the rusty fire escape.

This would have been bad news for a whole host of reasons, probably the very least of which was that my name was painted on that window: **Crag Banyon**. Yeah, that's me. Don't ask. Underneath my name, stenciled in black but faded as much as my name you could still make out **Private Investigations**. That's what occupied my time and kept the pantry stocked with bottles between my more momentous al fresco drunks.

As far as bottles were concerned, I was having great luck finding them that Monday morning. The problem was finding one that hadn't been sucked dry.

I'd lined up my handy store from my bottom desk drawer on my blotter, empty and useless for anything except target practice. They clinked harmony with the clanking radiator as I slammed every drawer in search of a bottle that still held some life in it.

I own two file cabinets. One was filled with case files, the other existed exclusively to keep my booze backup neatly filed away under L-M, for Liver Medicine. When I checked, the booze cabinet too held nothing but empty bottles.

I'm not a big fan of Mondays, which is why I usually don't come into work until Wednesday (Tuesday can take a flying leap, too at Banyon Investigations, Inc.), but this Monday was giving cause to petition the calendar people to eliminate the day altogether and turn the extra hours over to Saturday night around closing time, where everyone with half-a-pickled-brain knows they could be put to far better use.

Panic setting in, I skipped the other spots around the office where I stashed a bottle here and there, and went straight for the closet.

There wasn't a drop in the five cases I'd stowed behind my galoshes. This was my Apocalypse-is-nigh stockpile that I'd shoved in there a couple months back, right after those Arab-trained sea monsters flopped out of the Potomac and ripped the Jefferson Memorial up by its marble roots. Everybody went batshit about emergency preparedness back then, snatching up tons of bottled water, canned goods and batteries. The grocery stores were madhouses. Or so I'm told. I'd found the liquor store was in and out, service with a smile, no wait. Hey, don't knock it. If some Leviathan from the ocean's depths is going to swallow me whole, what good are Spaghetti-O's and batteries? I don't want Sigmund pissed so that he chews thirty-two times out of spite just because some can of Campbell's Cream of Celery I threw at him got stuck in one of his million eyes. I'd much rather be loaded off my ass and loose on my way down his gullet. And anyway, all the crazy hoarding preparation had been unnecessary. The Marines found the sea monsters chowing down on some Canadian tourists on a beach in Virginia and blasted them all to hell. Semper fi, rah-rah and go team. But that was then and this was now and where was my booze?

"Doris!" I bellowed.

Doris Staurburton was my secretary and sometimes girlfriend.

Check that. She was my sometimes-secretary, too. I saw the janitor around the office more often than Doris, and he'd been dead for eight years. He still came in sometimes, floating around with a spectral broom and trying to change light bulbs that his fingers passed right through. Guy was a moron when he was alive, and being dead hadn't upped the wattage in his ghostly brain. Still, like I said, even as a goddamn ghost he managed to occasionally drift in to work. On the other hand, there was Doris. She came in so rarely that if it wasn't for the photo of herself she'd had taken at the Space Needle on some vacation that was on her desk in the outer office, the booze would have done to my memory of her bleached-blonde beehive and puckered red kisser the same tabula rasa number it had done on my ex-wife. God bless alcohol.

As soon as I yelled, someone hopped-to in the outer room. It wasn't Doris who stuck her head around the door. For one thing he was shorter. The little guy in the neat, green business suit barely reached the knob. For another thing he was a he.

"Miss Doris isn't here, Mr. Crag."

The elf's name was Mannix. He worked around the office and sometimes helped out on cases. Crag Banyon Investigations was an equal opportunity employer. Every misfit loser that stumbled in off the street.

"What do you mean, she isn't here? That sure as hell wasn't zombie Marilyn Monroe doing Doris' ritual grooming when I walked by five minutes ago."

Even if the little guy was a halfway decent liar, I knew up close and personal that one would've been a crock. I'd just come back from a case in Haiti a month ago. I was an eyewitness when the zombie Candle in the Wind had been decapitated by that torch-wielding mob of autograph hounds in Port-au-Prince. I'd seen a week later that her head had sold for three hundred grand on eBay. Some sick bastard movie producer in L.A. It figured. There's a pervert born every minute, and that goes double for the Left Coast. My biggest regret was that I hadn't thought to store her noggin in my carry-on rather than dump it with the carrion. Turns out I got stiffed on the bill on that one *and* lost out on all that eBay Cloroxed head dough. Always the same crap luck for me, just on a new day.

I looked out into Doris' office and saw that the lipstick, eyeliner, rouge, compact, perfume, and the rest of the Macy's cosmetics counter that had been spread out on her blotter was gone, as was my unfaithful Girl Friday.

"I'm sorry, Mr. Crag," Mannix said, with a helpless shrug. "She said she won't work another minute until you hire an exterminator."

"First off, *another* minute? Did hell freeze over and Doris actually work sixty straight seconds around here when I wasn't looking?"

Mannix was pretty much cheerful all the time. Despite this major character flaw, I still let him hang around. At that moment, his perpetual smile turned hardboiled and looked as if one good sock to the mush would crack it like an eggshell. The only part of his anatomy that moved were his tennis ball eyes, which darted to the door in search of an escape route. I knew that Mannix didn't want to speak ill of Doris. The elf liked pretty much everybody, including -- despite the fact that she made him do all her work and thought he was about as useful as yesterday's racing form -- Doris.

"I...that is, she..." Mannix said.

"Forget it, kid. Put your brain back in park. You're gonna drop the transmission."

Mannix visibly relaxed when I announced the subject officially dropped.

"What happened to my booze?" I demanded, jerking a thumb over my shoulder at the empty crates on the closet floor.

"I don't know, Mr. Crag," the elf said.

Mannix tensed right back up again when I took a giant rhetorical step back and picked up the subject I'd dropped two seconds before.

"You were standing right next to Doris when I told her that hiring an exterminator is up to the super. That slob Johansen is your pal. He hire somebody yet?"

Mannix did odd jobs around the building in exchange for a free basement apartment in an old cramped coal bin. Johansen was a real prince.

"Mr. Bob said he's narrowing down his choices," the elf said.

"Choices my ass, the cheap bastard just doesn't want to shell out so much as a nickel to clean them out of here. There's a hundred exterminators in the yellow pages. That tub of guts Johansen hasn't called one because he's hoping he dies of a heart attack before everyone in the building comes down with plague. You know, Mannix, I haven't forgotten he has keys to every office in this dump. He's probably the thief who pounded down all my cough syrup."

"I don't think Mr. Bob drinks," Mannix said.

"Bull. One of which, in case you didn't know, he eats daily for breakfast along with about a million eggs and a trough of hash browns. A guy on the Pac-Man diet needs something to wash it all down." I had one bottle in my hand, which I held up to Mannix. There wasn't so much a single drop in the bottom. I tossed it in disgust to my sofa. "So what's eating Doris that she suddenly wants an exterminator?" I sighed. "When they showed up out of the blue two weeks ago she was insisting the little bastards were cute."

Mannix brought me out to my secretary's desk. The smooching photo of Doris had been joined by a second frame that looked as if it had been scavenged from the garbage chute. The wood was chipped and there was a definite odor of fish. Vincetti, the downstairs fishmonger, was supposed to dump his trash in the barrels out back, but heads and guts always somehow managed to make it into the building's common trash.

The rendering of Doris in the dirty frame wasn't too bad, considering they'd done it mostly in raw macaroni and glitter. I figured the fact that they'd elected to depict her in the buff was the reason she'd dumped her cosmetics collection back into her Louis Vuitton bag and hightailed it back for home.

It looked as if someone had scattered a handful of steroid-pumped caraway seeds all around the pictures on Doris' desk. Most significantly, there were two caps from Jack Daniels bottles representing the two most prominent features of Doris' anatomy glued to the picture. And that's when I knew where all my booze went.

"Get that fat bastard Johansen on the phone," I snapped.

"Yes, sir, Mr. Crag, sir," Mannix said, scampering obediently into Doris' chair.

He began spinning the rotary dial on the phone. I wasn't blind. The elf was flicking numbers at random. He also had his thumb on the cradle. Mannix was a sweet kid, but a crummy con artist.

"Mannix, since I have not yet drunk myself blind, if you're going to pretend to call somebody while I'm standing right in front of you, you have a better shot fooling me if you accidentally drop a pencil and unplug the cord from the wall first. Just an FYI for next time. In the meantime, thumb off the cradle and make the damn call."

"Oh, I'm sorry," the elf said. He lifted his little thumb and while I could hear the dial tone this time, he still didn't call Johansen. "Mr. Crag, do you think it's a good idea to call him a fat...naughty word?" he asked, once more flipping random numbers.

"Johansen *is* a fat bastard," I said. "I'm a firm believer in truth in advertising, Mannix. And you've dialed about thirty numbers. If the Vladivostok Taco Bell picks up, the call is coming out of your paycheck."

Mannix tapped the cradle and this time made no pretense of dialing. "That might be another reason to not call Mr. Bob right now," he suggested. "The office rent is overdue and if you call him a fat naughty word now, he might not be very jolly."

"See that?" I said, pointing to the scattering of what wasn't caraway seeds on my MIA secretary's desk. "You want to see unjolly, Mannix, wait'll you see me armed, sober and with a head full of terminal hantavirus giving me the unrestricted thrill of having absolutely nothing to lose."

The building had been overrun with mice for the past two weeks and no one could explain why. Vincetti's For the Halibut Fish Bazaar on the first floor was no more colossally unsanitary than it had been for the past decade, so no change there. And if anything was going to draw rodents to my cheap brownstone it was that health code violating fish guts smorgasbord downstairs. Yet no mice at all until two weeks before, and now they were stampeding through the halls like Patton's Third Army.

Myron Wasserbaum, the dentist SOB down the hall, had patients canceling appointments left and right, and finally for a reason other than his rancid breath or rank incompetence. The afternoon class at Madame Carpathia's Dance Studio at the back of the top floor the previous week had tap-tapped its shrieking way down the fire escape and when it hit the street did a heavily improvised syncopated version of the French infantry on maneuvers. For two weeks I'd seen the little buggers running around my office floor every time I flicked on the lights, but up until then I'd ignored them like I did the pink elephants I'd sometimes see doing handstands in the elevator after a particularly productive weekend of murdering brain cells. But this was now serious business.

"They're coming in here in broad daylight," I told Mannix. "They're crapping all over the place, they're scaring off my secretary with this creepy macaroni love letter--" I grabbed up the naked cartoon picture of Doris from her desk and returned it to the trash barrel from whence it had come, "--and more important than anything else, they've pounded down every drop of my booze. On a *Monday*. I've got a client coming in in twenty minutes and now I'm going to have to meet him sober. I *hate* meeting new people sober, Mannix. I much prefer a pleasant alcoholic delirium which affords a hazy romanticism while dulling the harsh edges of asshole reality."

I would have sent Mannix out on an emergency liquor run, but it wound up there wasn't time. Turns out the client was twenty minutes early. The air around the front door suddenly distorted like a funhouse mirror and Mannix and I were no longer alone.

I'm not a big fan of anything that can do the amazing appearing-disappearing, presto-chango bit. Anything that pops through a locked door while I'm sitting on the john is just begging for a lead corsage. But this joker looked harmless enough.

At first glance he was over eight feet tall, but at second glance I saw that a quarter of that was hat. He whipped off the long chapeau, the pointed end of which could've put an eye out. The hat was dark blue and covered with yellow stars and moons, just like the oversize bathrobe that dangled below his ankles. When he took a step, his hem dragged mouse droppings in his wake. I barely caught a glimpse of curly-toed yellow boots.

The guy was pale. So pale he looked like he'd lobster-up if he ever ventured out into sunlight for all of two seconds, which was probably why the brim on his hat was as big as a manhole cover. He had a wiry white beard that was bundled up at the braided end and tucked into his leather belt.

"Yes, hello, yes," he announced, in a raspy voice that sounded as if speaking was something he'd tried once in the hazy mists of youth but didn't enjoy and so kicked the habit. When he smiled, I saw the same thing could be said about dental hygiene.

"Mr. Crag Banyon, I presume?" A bony hand extended from the billowing sleeve of his oversized robes. "Merlin's the name. Call me Merle. There's a good chap."

The wizard didn't need to introduce himself, and knew it. He was just being polite. Even people around town whose only interest in royalty was ordinarily reserved for the tiny kings and queens that came tucked away in decks of fifty-two playing cards -- which included yours truly -- had been subjected to a total immersion royalty course the past couple of weeks. The Queen of Albion was visiting the city, and for days the *Gazette* had been wall-to-wall "royal watch" crapola. If I was a thirteen year old girl or a fat housewife I might have been thrilled. As a middle-aged heterosexual male, I had about as much use for royalty factoids as zit cream.

As assiduously as I'd avoided the news I'd still caught Merlin's mug on the front page, most recently on the paper that someone had dropped the day before on the floor of the men's room at O'Hale's Bar. In real life he looked pretty much the same as he did in black and white. I wasn't sure if he'd think that was a compliment or an insult, but when you're a thousand year old wizard you probably don't care one way or the other. It's not like he was pasting newspaper articles about himself in his wizard scrapbook.

The guy was part of the Queen of Albion's advance team, and he'd called the office that morning to ask for an appointment. Doris, who was as high on all this royalty bullshit as every other ditzy dame with no life in town, had called me at home shrieking that I'd better get to the office pronto for the most important meeting of my life. I figured she meant an AA meeting and I told her if she wanted to stage an intervention she could do it at O'Hale's Bar and that the first round was on me, but she just started blabbing on about the Queen and Merlin, and I knew I wouldn't get a minute's peace if I didn't go into work on a goddamn Monday. And in one of those great ironic twists that life loves to shaft me with, I was stuck in the office with the Queen of Albion's advance team wizard while Doris, whose fault it was I was there, was at that precise moment running like hell to the corner bus stop to escape some lovesick rat wannabes.

"May we talk in private?" Merlin asked. Without an invitation from me, he swept through the outer office and into my inner sanctum.

"Call Johansen," I ordered Mannix. "Tell him either those mice and their creepy folk art are gone by the end of the week or I'm rigging a can of Cheese Whiz to blow up down his aircraft carrier-size sweatpants and ringing the dinner bell." I headed back into my office and shut the door behind me.

The radiator was still clanking up a storm. Merlin stood over it, rubbing his hands together to warm the ancient sticks of bone. His hat was hanging on my coat rack along with my trench coat and fedora. Guy made himself right at home.

I took my seat behind my desk. He stayed at the radiator.

"If your hotel room's cold, I can have it sent over."

The wizard straightened up and glided over to the chair in front of my desk. "I spent a few centuries as a tree once," Merlin said. "You don't know cold until you've stood out there, naked of leaves, half-bent under snow. Dreadful business. Ah, yes, business. I haven't forgotten. No need to interrupt. We want to hire you."

He reached inside his robes, fumbled around a little, and produced a ruby as fat as an extra-large chicken egg. He sat the jewel on the edge of my desk.

"This is a cash business," I informed him. "You have that converted into U.S. tender, I might consider taking your case."

"Oh, it's not a case. Not a case, per se. No, no. We wish to hire you for her majesty's security detail."

I leaned back in my chair. "What do you need me for? I saw that entourage of hers shepherding her from the airport on TV last night. Half the houses on the west side were busted into while that was going on. It was open season once every crook in town saw every cop in town leading that coach down Highland Boulevard."

The Queen's coach was a giant bulletproof glass slipper drawn by eight white stallions. In the two hundred-plus years she'd been Queen, the horses had been replaced thirteen times but except for the bulletproofing which was added in the 1980s the carriage was essentially the same one she'd ridden in to her coronation in 1798. (That factoid was courtesy *Entertainment Tonight*, which goddamned Ed Jaublowski, the barkeep at O'Hale's had left on three nights before when he lost the knob to the TV in a vat of macaroni salad. I'd already informed Jaublowski that he owed me a free gallon of whatever 100 proof lighter fluid it'd take to kill that useless nugget of information.)

"Ah, the police," Merlin said. "Yes, the police. Well, the police are all well and good, aren't they, of course. But we like to rely not solely on the local constabulary. We hire private consultants as well. Fellows with their ears closer to the ground, that sort of thing. Our advance people checked, and you're the top man."

That was true. I'm the top P.I. in town, at least according to the yellow pages. I was number two for years, until Alvin Abergnon of Abergnon AAA-1 Security Agency took a round of buckshot to the belly on a cheating husband case two years ago.

"So what's the job? You want me to check with my snouts around town and see if anybody has it in for Her Royal Handbag?"

"Snouts?" Merlin asked.

"Informants," I explained. "Only a few of them have actual snouts."

"Ah, colloquialism. Lovely. No. We want you up at the podium. Put your face right out there for everybody to see. We find that detectives mix more comfortably with a certain class of, shall we say, *people* that local constabulary never does. If these, for lack of a better term, *people* see one of their own on the squad, they stay back. You're another layer of protection."

He began fussing at the knees of his robes, picking at a strand of thread with long, bony fingers. There seemed to be something he was keeping to himself, but that was always the case with clients. If everybody was honest, I'd be out of a job.

"That's the theory anyway," Merlin continued. "Personally, I don't see the why. But we do what we do, more out of habit these days." He tapped the ruby with a fingertip that was so pale it was vaguely blue. "Pays well."

"Listen, buddy, if you want to pay me for doing nothing, count me in. If nothing else I'll get a firsthand look at my ex-wife's life-long alimony vacation. But like I said up front, that needs to be cashed in for real American dough."

Merlin scooped up the ruby as he got to his feet. "Be at the Albion embassy in an hour," he said. "Your money and instructions will be waiting for you there. Fellow by the name of Jeeves is directing the lot. I'm just a hired hand these days, I'm afraid."

"Can't do today," I said. "Make it tomorrow. I misplaced my best liver and I have to see if it's turned up in the lost and found at O'Hale's Lemonade Stand."

"One hour," Merlin insisted. "The job is this afternoon."

I gave a narrow-eyed stare into his watery blue peepers. "Hiring me at eleven in the morning for a gig this afternoon? That's pretty short notice."

"The, ah, gentleman who was hired originally was injured. Nothing to do with us. Fell down some stairs at his office. Broke a leg or something, I understand."

"Right," I said. "So what you're saying is Miss America couldn't fulfill her duties so you're promoting the next pretty swimsuit in line."

"Yes, essentially," Merlin said. "Is there a problem?"

"How much is that rock worth?"

"I'm not sure," said the wizard, holding the ruby to the light. "In today's market, I would guess somewhere better than two thousand dollars, American."

"Excuse me while I dig out my best bikini."

"Ah, excellent. In the meantime…" He reached inside his robes and removed a book, which he slapped down on the surface of my desk. "Background reading."

A much younger version of the Queen of Albion was etched on the cover of the leather-bound book.

The wizard plucked his hat off the coat rack and returned it to his head. He'd mentioned earlier that he'd spent time as a tree and I could see it now. The hat gave him an added teetering two feet of height, the wrinkled hem of his robe spread like gnarled roots across the office floor and his gangly arms like crooked branches.

I poked a cautious finger at the book, nudging it an inch across the battle-scarred surface of my cheap oak desk. It looked a lot less Zane Grey than my usual speed. I was going to tell the wizard to give me the Cliff's Notes version, but the air around Merlin suddenly twisted, as if the old codger was a facecloth that the hands of some unseen giant was wringing water out of, and just like that he was gone.

The door to my office opened and Mannix stuck his head inside. "Do we have a case?" the little eavesdropper asked.

"Did you call fatso Johansen?" I countered.

Without a word, Mannix disappeared back into the outer office.

I pinned the book to my desk with the tip of my index finger and reluctantly dragged it towards me. It was thinner than I initially thought, and the etching of the Queen of Albion on the leather cover looked like it had been carved back in the early 1800s. I used the same cautious finger to flip open the cover.

Once Upon A Time...

Four words into it and I was already bored. The taskmasters at P.S. 104 hadn't gotten me to do homework through eleven years of grammar school and I wasn't about to start now. Whatever background information I needed, I'd pick up along the way.

I tossed the book to the sofa across the room where it landed on an arm rather than the cushion I'd been aiming for, slipped off and tipped into the closet where it banged against a case of rattling empty bottles.

"Keep it down out there!" an angry and tiny high-pitched voice squeaked from inside the wall. A dozen hungover squeaks beyond the baseboard slurred agreement.

Chapter 2

Embassy Row was over on Fourth and Polk near the old abandoned horse smelting plant. The buildings were mostly Victorian era numbers, with all the cornices, carriage houses and widow's walks you'd expect. Or so the rumors said. You couldn't really see any of them very clearly from the street. During the Forties and Fifties, when the huge old houses were bought up and converted to use as embassies for various foreign greaseballs and harp pluckers, high brick walls were constructed around each of them. From the air, the whole block looked like one of those multi-box mail cubicles behind the receptionist's desk at every high school around the country. From the street, all I could see was the sharp right angle of wall meeting sidewalk, with the occasional wrought iron weathervane sticking into the clouds a million miles above my head.

The weathervane above the Albion embassy was a chorus line of cows linked arm-in-arm and stomping like Rockettes across a pulverized Frenchman. I guessed the cows were symbolic of the ritual criminal acts that Albion chefs regularly perpetrated against the bovine species. The dead Frenchman symbolized a dead Frenchman.

I recognized the guard at the gate from the Beefeater Gin label. He wore a red coat, hat and tights and -- once he'd checked my I.D. and called in to the embassy -- waved me through with a flick of the nosegay on the tip of his spear.

There was a lion in a cage inside the gate with his ass backed up to the wall and his tail hanging through to the outside. I'd seen it wagging out on the sidewalk side, but I was an invited guest and so I didn't have to ring the royal bell.

I'd shown up at lunchtime. The grounds reeked of boiled beef and batter-fried fish. The kitchen staff was in the process of marinating supper.

A small dragon was staked in the front yard and the animal was snapping its massive jaws at servants in white coats. I couldn't blame it for being ticked, since the servants were hurling bottles at the dragon from a safe distance. The bottles shattered on its scaly back, which glistened as streams of liquid carried glass shards down to under its belly, dripping onto the grass. The sharp stink of gallons of Worcestershire sauce assaulted my nostrils. The animal roared and spun, crunching shards of shattered glass beneath its clawed feet, and nearly caught one of the kitchen help with a blast of fiery breath. As it was, the servant had to strip off his singed coat and stomp out the flames at the hem. A much younger servant rushed forward with a fresh white coat, which the older gentleman shrugged on. Impeccably dressed once more, he resumed shattering bottles of sauce on the dragon's back.

The whole performance was carried out in the very efficient, very bloodless, very Albion manner the world associated with the island nation. You could keep a Popsicle frozen by sticking it up an Albionman's ass, not to mention it'd taste better than the cow's head with beet gravy his wife was boiling up for supper.

"Banyon," announced a voice as crisp as snapping celery.

He was bald and old, with a microscopic fringe of close-cropped gray hair to break up the monotony between his ears. He wore pinstriped pants and a waistcoat. At least I think it was a waistcoat. I don't see many waistcoats on the Salvation Army rack where I do my finest suit shopping. He had the largest pores I'd ever seen on a human, probably to vent the stink of a lifetime of Albion cuisine. He smelled vaguely of curry mixed with a couple thousand internal organ meat pies.

The short man held a clipboard, a gold pen and a fat envelope. The envelope he handed over to me. "Four thousand, American," he sniffed.

"That's more than my usual fee," I said as I counted out the cash. I didn't bother to tell him that it was double what Merlin said the ruby was worth or that my normal clientele usually paid in countless lies, worthless IOUs, itemized bills unopened and marked "return to sender," restraining orders and occasionally gunfire. I further failed to mention that the heartache of going unpaid by my deadbeat clients always ended with me drunk and broke at O'Hale's.

"We flatter ourselves that we are not your usual clientelle," the snoot said, as if he'd read my mind. He offered a yellow-toothed smirk.

Merlin wasn't kidding. His name was Jeeves. He had some cockamamie title that he told me to impress me and which I tried to forget before he'd even finished, but which he managed to work into his introduction four times. Jeeves was Albion High Whizboom for Her Majesty's External Matters, which he told me meant that his stiff upper lip quivered alone at the top of the food chain of the Queen of Albion's entourage.

As I was being unimpressed by his title, there was a sudden murmur among the footmen and carriage drivers in the great cobbled driveway of the Albion embassy. Even the kitchen staff risked death by dragon barbecue to stop marinating and stand at attention. I followed the gaze of one of the nearby beefeater guards, and there she was.

The Queen of Albion stood on a balcony on the third floor of the embassy. She wore long gloves to her elbows. A blue purse hung off her left forearm. The tiara in her 1950s Donna Reed hairdo glinted, and a simple string of pearls hung down to the collar of her blue dress. The two hundred year old broad wasn't looking down at the grounds or her many servants. She was staring at the city beyond the walls.

"So that's the dame herself, is it?" I said. "Think I should run up and say hi?"

"Yeeeees," Jeeves said, drawing out the word like a dog offering a low growl of warning over a fresh ham bone. He kept one eye trained on the Queen as he spoke. "You're joking, of course. Frightfully clever. You will *not* be meeting the Queen."

I was pretty sure I wouldn't be at that moment, since Her Royal Runtness turned quietly around and disappeared back inside the embassy.

"Too bad," I said. "I was hoping she'd share tips on how to remove stubborn mutton stains. Wisk just doesn't seem to cut it for the tapestries in my john."

I could see Jeeves didn't like me. So mission accomplished there.

The Albion High Whizboom informed me that the Queen was having a meet-and-greet late that afternoon with a bunch of local bigwigs at St. Regent's Drive-Thru Cathedral. I was to stand at the front of the stage looking real pretty-like for the cameras, and for that I'd walk away with a cool four grand.

"Do you understand why, Mr. Banyon?" Jeeves asked.

"According to Merlin, so the scum of the city know there's someone standing between them and the Queen who doesn't give two shits about Miranda warnings or charges of police brutality. Oh, unpucker your ass, Jeeves, those are my words, not his."

"Yes," Jeeves droned. He gave me a look like I'd slipped grapefruit juice into his shepherd's pie. "Essentially correct, if inelegantly phrased. You've been paid, and you have your assignment. Your ride is here. Good day, Mr. Banyon."

I got the distinct impression that I didn't have to worry about trading Christmas cards with his Grand Tight-Assness. That was it for the big meeting. Jeeves waved forward an embassy pumpkin that sped me across town to St. Regent's.

The Cathedral District was four blocks in a crummy part of town that I'd once walked as a beat cop. The church cast a massive, spiked shadow over all the decaying tenements, gin joints and pool parlors that squatted along the dank streets far below its highest steeple. It was the largest cathedral the Church of Albion managed in America, and it was loaded up with dozens of spires, a couple hundred flying buttresses, and a stained glass window for nearly every page of the bible including copyright and footnotes. If all the granite slabs that had gone into its construction were stacked on top of one another, St. Regent's would form a tower tall enough to actually reach God. And if I was the poor SOB they shoved up to the top to meet the big guy I'm sure He'd be out to lunch with Buddha and Ra for the next thousand years, and on the climb back down to Earth I'd get snatched by Moon Men and put to work as a slave pasteurizer in their lunar cheese caves. (Yeah, I know that's what happened to that guy over in Flagstaff back in the Nineties, but unlike him I'd wind up dead of Jarlsberg poisoning in a brie pit at the bottom of the Sea of Tranquility and not on *Oprah* with a national bestseller. Trust me.)

The cops had already set up roadblocks around St. Regent's. They'd done the stuff you see in movies: removed mail boxes, sealed manholes, rousted the bums that were always hanging around the sidewalk in front of the soup kitchen next door. I didn't need my old cop's gut feeling to know that the place was locked down tighter than a Washington madam's little black book. The Queen needed me for her protection like a whale needed a shotgun and a box of soggy shells to bag some plankton for brunch.

A stage had been set up in the side yard of the cathedral. Nice shrubs, nice grass, and a few nice tents set up with chairs and tables beneath them. A regular Ricky Nelson garden party. A work crew was putting the finishing touches on a wooden dais that had been built snug up to the moss-covered granite side wall of the church.

It was a good thing I wasn't expecting a happy hello. A plainclothes cop with a sour mug and a couple of Pony Express-level bags under his bloodshot eyes caught one look at me and yelled to the rest of the flatfoots within shouting distance.

"Hey, great! Banyon's here. We can all go home, fellas, the cavalry's arrived!"

Actually, as greetings by Detective Daniel Jenkins went, that mound of steaming sarcasm fell into the top ten most civil ones I'd ever received. If I'd been a twelve year old girl I'd've rushed right home to record the momentous moment in my diary. Instead I pulled out a hip flask, took a swig, then capped it an inch from the flatfoot's nose.

"I'd offer you a snort, Jenkins, but alcohol impairs judgment and going by that suit it's obvious yours is already hanging by a polyester thread."

"Just stay out of my way, Banyon. The *real* police have jobs to do."

"So why'd they bring you along? If they're that busy, they should've just locked you in your office with copies of the *Gazette* spread on the floor 'til they got back."

I've turned Jenkins a whole box of Crayola colors over the years, nearly all of them subtle shades of red and purple. I was a little disappointed that I only managed to get his puss to flush a dark pink. I was hoping for at least maroon, but the Queen's visit apparently had him too distracted.

"Just get out of here, Banyon," Jenkins snarled. "I don't know what you're doing here this early anyway. The Queen isn't due to arrive for another three hours, and you don't have anything to do even when she gets here."

"Oh, I got plenty to do, Jenkins. The best P.I. in town is getting paid four grand just to look pretty for the cameras."

I did the whole chest-puffing thing. You know, like a real A-one jerk-ass. I figured it had to gall my old bosom pal Detective Dan Jenkins that I'd been picked as the cream of the crop of my worthless profession. As it turned out he was a lot less P.O.'ed than this P.I. had imagined.

Jenkins only smirked. "Oh, yeah, the *best. That's* why you're here, Banyon. Just stay out of my hair." The radio in his pocket suddenly squawked to life, and he fished it out and began shouting at the cop on the other end. "No, you don't need snipers on the roof of Woolworth's, Crandelle," he snapped. "It's low and on the wrong end of the block. Pull everyone off there and draw in tighter to the cathedral. Over!"

Jenkins wandered off, so I didn't hear whatever it was Officer Crandelle replied beyond a little muffled static about a family of pterodactyls roosting on the Blanchard Building which was on the Queen's travel route between Embassy Row and St. Regent's.

I only gave a moment of curious thought as to why I hadn't managed to ruffle Jenkins' feathers. It must have been because he'd already known I was coming, since the embassy would have had to clear me with the local cops.

At that moment the Archbishop, who was a sometimes client, appeared on the side lawn and when the little fat holy roller with the rum-blossomed face spotted me and motioned me over, I did the same thing everyone who's ever met Dan Jenkins does with the experience: I put the annoying flatfoot bastard out of my mind.

# # #

The caterers were first to arrive an hour and a half later. The kitchen help I'd seen at the embassy was right behind them in a horse-drawn pumpkin, and they directed the chaos in white coats and matching red cravats.

The centerpiece was the dragon. I don't know from fancy cooking, which puts me in the same camp as every Albion housewife with a mixing spoon, a goat's bladder and a cup of tarragon for seasoning. Beats me why they don't just serve supper in the bathroom with a side order of Charmin to save time.

The dragon looked like it was cooked right, at least to my untrained eye. I'd seen Julia Child do one once, and it looked pretty much the same. (That was before she became a zombie and every episode turned into different variations on preparing raw brains for six. How The French Zombie Chef is still on the air, I'll never know. Goddamn PBS.)

The dragon was on its back on a huge platter, slit from chin to pelvis and steaming from the inside out. The internal temperature of a living dragon can get up to something like five hundred degrees, at least according to a *National Geographic* article at my barber's. Dead, the thing was like a big can of open Sterno, with fire licking like twin tiki torches from both nostrils. The eyes had been replaced with shaved coconuts with cherries embedded dead center for that festive, still-alive look. I guess. Don't ask me. In my book, food doesn't look back at you. The day Sandy's Diner starts including the cow's eyes in their double-stack burgers is the day I go fruity vegetarian.

The rest of the tables in the buffet tent were standard Albion fare. Boiled sheep heads, boiled cow intestines, boiled horse rectums and steaming tureens of boiled turnips, beets and parsnips. All the water they'd abused to cook supper could have floated the USS *Missouri* from here to Guadalcanal.

Dignitaries had slowly started to arrive not long after the kitchen help, and the rows of chairs in front of the stage were filling up with suits and gowns. I spotted the mayor and his wife, along with the new chief of police. I didn't know the guy; he had taken over running the cops after my old boss, Chief Strett, retired two years before. The new chief kept a hairy eyeball on me up near the stage as he made the rounds with the business and political leaders who had shown up for the Queen's first stop in the country.

There had been reporters there all along, mostly cooling their heels. But as the long shadows of late afternoon stretched dark fingers across the weary city, I saw more and more cameras switching on. The babe field reporter -- Kelli-something -- from Channel 16 set up with her camera crew near me, but she didn't point camera lens, eyes, or considerable rack in my direction. The news people were focusing all their attention on the stage where the Queen would be taking a load off the royal hoofs.

At about quarter to five, Jeeves and his bald head wended through the crowd and caught up with me where I was lounging near the stage.

"Try to look professional, Mr. Banyon," the Albion High Whizboom insisted.

"Try to look like you've got hair," I suggested. "And why are you alone? Where the hell is Merlin? I figured he'd be in the middle of this mess somewhere."

I thought the wizard would be there as part of the advance team, but I hadn't seen his pointy hat anywhere in the growing crowd all afternoon.

"Never mind that," the Albion official informed me. "Never mind, never mind. The Queen's motorcade has left the embassy. Her Royal Highness will be here in four minutes. Hurry, hurry. Take your position, Mr. Banyon."

In his tails and vest and with that glazed Albion upper crust expression the guy looked as cool as a tray of ice cubes in the back of a polar bear's freezer, but when he turned to check the gate I spotted a thin line of sweat glistening on his quivering lip.

The Queen and her entourage must have had a good tail wind and run every stop sign, because Jeeves' four minutes was actually closer to one. Jeeves nearly jumped out of his penguin suit a moment later when the Queen's motorcade passed through the gates and into the long driveway beside St. Regent's.

The vehicles were mostly sedans and limos, with a few police motorcycles thrown in for good measure. There were also a few enchanted carriages in the mix. Those things always run like crap, and these were no different. They were dumping enough magical fairy dust from their tailpipes to give a case of phony glitter lung to every city worker union slug who'd have to sweep the streets the next day. A private American citizen in a restored flying Edsel would've been slapped with a million in fines by the EPA and the state environmental cops if they'd spewed that much tinsel into the air. Rank, royalty and diplomatic plates had its privilege. So much for the classless society.

The Queen's glass slipper coach was a few cars back and I noted that not one of the ten thousand cops present whipped out a ticket book when the royal horses parked across four handicapped spaces and the lead horse took a dump on the parish azaleas.

The side of the glass slipper swung open, a set of invisible stairs unfolded, and the Queen of Albion stepped down to the driveway.

She looked the same as she did on TV and on the balcony back at the embassy. The fact was, she didn't look any different from any of the nice old broads who met Tuesdays downstairs for the St. Regent's Ladies Sodality Bingo Nite. She was squat, old, gray-haired, and was now wearing a matching hat to go along with her plain blue dress. A blue veil with wide mesh extended from the large brim of the hat over her eyes and down as far as her nose. The simple set of white pearls matched her long gloves as well as the frilly white collar of her blue dress. A nice old dame, maybe, but sure as hell not impressive enough to make me throw out my bum knee curtseying.

The Queen waved that little queenly wave of hers and men from the cars swarmed her and led her up the stairs to the dais.

"Stay here, Banyon," Jeeves hissed, before hustling up the stairs to join the rest of the Queen's frou-frou entourage.

I knew something was wrong when I took my post at ground level, front and center, below the stage. I was all alone. I figured the cops would pull in to form a cordon around the stage, but they continued to man posts in the crowd and near the fence, with a heavy concentration near the main gate. I caught sight of a couple of sharpshooters on nearby roofs, but there was no police presence near or on the stage itself.

The mayor gave a welcome speech. Some stale boilerplate about shared culture and shared language. The kind of useless political fluff that gets you nine terms in office and hot and cold running mistresses, paid for with tax dollars and passed off as assistants.

The Archbishop gave a little hello of his own, welcoming the Supreme Governess of the Church of Albion to his personal little corner of Heaven's waiting room.

As for me, I had my eyes peeled on anything and everything. If something happened up on that stage, I was the only one near enough to do anything about it. I didn't know if that was by design or due to incredibly inept handling of Her Queenship's security. With Detective Dan Jenkins in charge, I was inclined to think it was the latter. The why didn't matter. All my attention was focused getting through the next couple of hours until the Queen was safely back in her bulletproof glass shoe.

It turned out I didn't get through the next couple of minutes.

The final greeting was delivered by the Viceroy of Fiddlesticks, an old friend of the royal family who kept a summer place for butterfly strangling out on Rough Islands. As his mustache was being spooled back inside his iron lung, the Queen got to her sensible pumps. A hush descended on the crowd of gathered misfits and suck-ups as the old gal stepped up to the podium.

The Queen gave the crowd a satisfied little smile, as if she was very slowly breaking wind.

"We are pleased to be in America once more," the Queen of Albion announced, in that high-pitched, robotic voice of hers. That was as far as she got.

It was the falling mortar that I caught sight of first. It hit the stage and scattered in a soft rat-tat-tat, like a handful of tossed Orville Redenbacher kernels. A couple of blue bouffants started to gather tiny chunks of mortar dandruff, like the first snowflakes of a storm gathering on the hood of a parked car. Small bits of stone landed on the shoulders of dignitaries who swept the pieces away like nuisance flies. The largest piece bounced right past the Queen and rolled off the edge of the stage, landing in the grass at my feet.

I was the first to look up, and so I was the first to see the chunk of granite tearing loose from high up on the cathedral's roof.

It might have been a good thing the mice had drunk all my booze. Even sober (or at least marginally so) I was surprised I still had it in me.

There was a shout from the crowd. Eyes began to turn skyward. A scream. Before the place erupted in pandemonium an instant later, I was already shoulder rolling up onto the stage. When the real panic came, I was on my feet and running.

Men and women at the back of the stage jumped from their seats. The crowd out in front of the stage ran shrieking for the buffet tents and the main gate.

All around me, the world suddenly grew dark, as if the late afternoon sun had gone bye-bye in an unscheduled solar eclipse. I felt the pressure of air compressing at my back and a whistling in my ears. Something heavy was flying in fast.

The Queen was still standing at the podium, looking up now, but with utter incomprehension in her eyes. She didn't seem even to see me as I raced up and scooped her up in both arms. For an old bird, she was surprisingly sturdy. I tucked her up like a two hundred year old pigskin and ran like hell for the stairs on the far side of the stage.

I didn't get two steps before the crash.

The stage buckled and chunks of wood splintered all around me. I was suddenly on the deck of an old wooden ship and the whole store of powder kegs had just gone boom in the armory. I caught the final intact plank like one of those skateboarding bastards on a railing at the mall, and I slid down to the stairs, hitting at a sprint and bounding down to the grass. I didn't stop running until I made it to the gravel of the driveway. I planted the Queen next to one of her white horses and wheeled around.

The chunk of granite had struck the stage in the precise spot where the old bag had been standing. The podium was gone; crushed to toothpicks, with the pieces shoved through to the grass below the stage. I saw the arched end of a flying buttress jutting out from the ruins of the stage like a giant beckoning finger, and when I looked up I saw that the eight buttresses that had lined the roof of St. Regent's for a century was minus one.

The cops finally showed up. I was shoved out of the way by Jenkins and his Keystone Kronies. The Queen's people were next, including a panicked Jeeves.

The royal horses were thrown into reverse and the Queen was hustled up inside her slipper. I hated to tell them that while the thing might be bulletproof, it wouldn't stop three tons of church from crushing it into a glass flip-flop. It didn't matter. The other seven remaining buttresses remained locked solidly in place high above.

No one, not even the news cameras, were paying any attention to yours truly.

"You know, thanks is kind of traditional in this country," I said. "It's fallen out of favor with the younger crowd, but some old timers still deploy it in extreme situations. Somebody saving the broad chosen by God to run your country from getting squashed like a squirrel on the interstate would probably count as one."

I made the announcement to anyone in the immediate vicinity who'd listen, but it was like I'd gone invisible.

The door to the slipper slammed shut and the coach and the rest of the cars and carriages beat a hasty retreat for the church gate and the street beyond. The reporters raced for vans and the news crews followed like a school of sharks; if sharks had no ethics, much smaller brains and could fit in a tanning booth.

No one seemed interested in the vacant spot high above where a multi-ton flying buttress that had almost pulverized the Queen of Albion had been torn loose, nor did they notice the massive, shadowy figure that at that moment crept from view at the edge of the roof and disappeared behind one of the lower spires.

Chapter 3

By the time I reached the roof ten minutes later, the courtyard far below was virtually empty of non-police personnel. There was some fussing still going on around the buffet tent. The Archbishop was arranging for the dragon and the rest of the food to be boxed up and sent to the homeless clown shelter over on Seltzer Drive.

I was alone on the wide walkway at the edge of the roofline.

If you didn't know that it was a two hundred foot drop to the ground, the level path on which I carefully picked my way was just another sidewalk beneath the long shadows of the flying buttresses that arched from the roof to my right up to a second wall that sprung up out of the roof to my left about twenty feet up.

It was the fifth buttress along that had been wrenched loose, and the empty space it left behind looked like the first missing tooth in a rookie hobo's mouth.

A very old inscription was carved on the wall below the buttress. There was Latin writing all over the cathedral, hacked into the granite when the place went up. There had clearly been several very old words chiseled into the wall, but all but one had been scratched out. The last remaining word was clear as a bell: VERITAS.

"Banyon, what the hell are you doing up here?" a voice snapped behind me.

"Settling a bet, Jenkins," I said, turning to the flatfoot who had just stepped onto the path through a door in one of the smaller spires. "Everyone down there swore you didn't know which way was up, but I was pulling for you. I knew you had to, what with your head spending so much time up your ass."

Jenkins didn't have time to retort. A police forensics team had just come through the door behind him. The three men and one woman were dressed in white jumpsuits and booties and carried portable labs and sample kits.

"It's a waste of time," Jenkins assured them, hitching his thumbs in his belt in his best impersonation of Barney Fife. "The dump is old. This butt dress thing just came loose on its own. I'm surprised more chunks of it aren't dropping to the street."

The remaining seven flying buttresses were solidly anchored and weren't going anywhere for centuries. I looked over the edge of the roof. The dais where the missing buttress had come to rest was not directly below the spot where the slab of granite had held up the roof, but was about twenty yards to the right, which meant it hadn't just dropped, it had been hurled at the spot where the Queen had been standing. Not to mention the fresh scratch marks in the granite obscuring all but one Latin word.

The sun had sunk low in the early evening sky. The roof of St. Regent's was one of the few spots high enough in town that sunlight still struck it. The gray of twilight had settled like a cold shroud to the city far below. And on a roof across the street, something very large stirred. I saw the shadow move, ducking from behind an air conditioning unit and moving at a swift crawl behind a fat tin air vent.

I hadn't been sure what I'd seen on the roof of St. Regent's minutes before, but I knew I was seeing the same shadowy figure crawling around on the roof of Woolworth's, from which Dan Jenkins, in his infinite wisdom, had pulled all the cops before the Queen's arrival. And this time, I was pretty sure I knew what I was looking at.

"You're just the gift that keeps on giving, aren't you, Jenkins?" I mused.

"Banyon, are you still here? Get off this roof. In fact, clear off the grounds. I don't need you polluting this scene any more than you already have."

"I'm nowhere near as polluted as I should be this time of day, Jenkins," I said, "so you don't need to tell me twice. See you in the funny pages. Don't trip and plummet to a horrible death or anything."

I'm always looking out for people like that. Albert Schweitzer's got nothing on me.

A dozen ladders and staircases later, I was back down in the cathedral driveway. The embassy pumpkin that had driven me there was gone. Not that it mattered. I still smelled vaguely of rotting pie, and I didn't need the ride anyway.

I trotted across the street and headed up the alley between Woolworth's and the Goodrich Tire Center.

I thought I'd have to climb up to the roof, but it turned out what I was after was already on its way down. The large black shadow I had seen skulking from one hiding spot to another was hanging from one giant hand and was in the process of swinging down to the alley floor. It landed with a thunderclap on two very large cloven hooves.

"What's a pretty thing like you doing slinking around dark alleys?" I asked.

The creature wheeled, all slavering fangs and giant glowing yellow eyes.

He was a towering, eight-foot figure wrapped in black leather skin. All over his misshapen body were crooked bones that threatened to poke through to the surface. The twin curved bones of his elbows looked viciously sharp as he flexed his biceps, and were just itching to bust through and do some serious damage. He was powerfully built and I guessed most souls who encountered the behemoth at the deep end of a dark alley figured they were about to get driven into the hard pavement like a croquet wicket. But when he saw me, his ragged black wings drew far in to his knobby spine, his shoulders sank, and his melon-sized eyes went from angry to a guilty weariness.

"Oh. Banyon. It's you."

"I should run inside and pick you up a tin badge and a toy gun. Your powers of observation are wasted as a civilian. You should take the cop exam." I gave him my beadiest glare. "Just what the hell do you think you're doing, Molokai?"

"Nothing," the demon said, like an innocent kid with a bat and glove standing next to a broken window with a baseball-sized hole in it. "Heading to work. Shortcut."

"So that wasn't you I saw hurling pieces of church at the Queen of Albion."

"Oh, is that today?" Molokai asked, turning up the phony innocent act. It fit him about as well as a size-four skirt in the Kmart Little Miss department.

"Drop the act, Molokai," I said. "I saw you up there. Then when I got up there, I saw you over here. Those wings might be crap for flying, but I'm betting they're good for a short flying squirrel glide from point A to point B. So you going to tell me why you tried to turn the

Queen into a mound of mashed potatoes or do I get the cops in here and let them break out the rubber hoses and Barbra Streisand records?"

"God, no!" Molokai begged, throwing up both hands in surrender. "I don't know why he had me do it. He just told me to throw it at her."

"Who?" I pressed.

"I don't know. Some human. I never saw him before."

"So you're in the habit now of doing favors for total strangers?"

"Not strangers, *stranger*. *One* human, *one* favor. And it wasn't even like a favor. I'm not big on charity, Banyon."

"Right. How much did he pay you?" Molokai slumped against the grimy Woolworth's loading dock. "Not one penny," he said glumly. "He threatened me. Said he had friends at Immigration. If I didn't do what he told me he said he'd report me and they'd deport me back to Hell. You know I can't go back there, Banyon. They'd chew me up and spit me out. Then they'd do it again, every day for a thousand years. And that'd only be the place-keeper until they could figure out a permanent punishment."

"How would a stranger know about your immigration status?"

"Beats me. I know people on this side now, Banyon. I've even helped *you* out from time to time. Word gets around."

"Hmm," I said, considering.

The demon jumped on my hesitation.

"I mean, think about it, Banyon. It's not like I *want* to call attention to myself hiding up on that church, do I? Why would I do that if someone hadn't made me? I couldn't say no to him. What other choice did I have?"

It was the same excuse offered by every no-good pissant punk for every stolen bike, boosted car or genocide the world over. Another minute and he'd be bawling that he was an altar boy in short pants back in demon Catholic school.

"What did this guy look like?" I asked.

Molokai shrugged and a few droplets of slime slipped from the tips of his wings and splattered to the loading dock. "I don't know. He was wearing a sweatshirt with the hood pulled up. I never got a good look at his face."

"What about scratching out everything on the wall but 'veritas?'"

Molokai lifted his hands, palms forward, and I got a good look at the claws that had scraped down the rest of the granite around the last Latin word.

"Just doing what he told me," the demon insisted. "What, you think now that I scratch up cathedrals and toss around buttresses for the hell of it? No way do I want people to know I live up there. You know that. Plus what do I need with a new hobby? I've already got one rolling hobos at the stockyard. Blame the guy, Banyon. He told me to remove everything but veritas, so I removed everything but veritas. Simple as that."

Ordinarily demons aren't big on the truth, so you've got to take everything they say with a huge grain of salt. But Molokai knew that I knew all about his illegal status, and he knew I was bastard enough to rat him out to INS if he was yanking my chain.

"You really due at work?" I asked.

He pushed off from the loading dock and stood up straight, a hopeful look in his giant eyes. "Night shift," he said, nodding vigorously.

"I won't turn you in. *Yet*," I warned. "You caught a break with the investigating cop. It's Jenkins. That flatfoot couldn't find wet in water, so he might never track you down. I've seen him have a hard time getting the pencil out of the maze on the kiddie placemat. But I'm warning you, Molokai, if you're lying I'm handing you over to the Feds and it's straight back to the pitchfork palace for you, capice?"

"Yeah, yeah," he said, nodding and backing away. "I got you. And I'm not lying. I've gone straight, Banyon, I swear."

"Right," I droned. "Get out of here before I change my mind."

Molokai turned and clomped away on those giant hooves of his. His sweeping tail knocked over six tin rubbish barrels in his haste to get around the corner and out of sight.

I looked back towards the street. The last of the day's dying sunlight brushed a few brilliant orange streaks across the topmost steeple of St. Regent's.

Somewhere in the dark below the glowing silver cross, Detective Dan Jenkins was ensuring that the investigation would move along as fast as the line at the DMV and be as incompetently run as an all-Eskimo volunteer fire engine.

I patted my pocket where I'd stuffed the envelope Jeeves had given me. The fat wad of four grand in cash practically screamed directions to the nearest hooch parlor.

I saw an article in the paper the previous week about a fancy-pants spa in Switzerland where you can go to have your conscience removed. But the procedure cost two hundred times what I had in my pocket, and long before I could manage to save up that kind of dough I was hoping regular daily doses of self-prescribed alcohol would have mine whittled away to just a nuisance nib. In the meantime, I was stuck with goddamn Jiminy Cricket on my shoulder.

"One quick stop, then O'Hale's," I said. "Cross my heart, boys." I patted the lump of bills that was burning through my breast pocket.

The last ray of sunlight fled the tip of the tallest steeple as I hustled down the alley toward the amber glow of the streetlights.

Chapter 4

I found the Albion Embassy where I'd left it. That could be a problem with some of these older buildings. My apartment building, for instance. It'd stay rooted to one spot for six months and then, poof. Gone. It took me a week to find it last time, clear on the other side of town. But it's rent controlled, so what are you gonna do? The gates were locked and all I had to talk to was the bell. I pulled the lion's tail that hung out through the hole in the wall, and I heard the royal animal roar on the other side. A new Beefeater Gin guard stuck his ruddy face up to the wrought iron.

"Whadda you want, mate?" he asked.

The guard's eyes were bloodshot and he weaved in place, using his spear as a two-handed prop to keep from pitching forward. Guy was drunk off his ass, which was no surprise. He was an Albionman and it was after five o'clock. Lucky bastard.

"Let me talk to Jeeves."

"We got forty of 'em 'ere," the guard slurred.

"Merlin then," I said. Might as well go straight for the top.

"Who?"

"Tall guy. Wizard. Dresses like a box of Lucky Charms."

"Oh, I 'eard of *that* Merlin, mate," the guard assured me. "Everyone knows Merlin." He scrunched up his face. "It's just that, what makes you think 'e's 'ere?"

I wasn't going to get any further with him on that front, so I rewound the conversation back to the start. "The Jeeves I'm looking for is the the boss of all the other ones. Polisher of the Royal Apple and King Whizbang of Efferling."

The guard got on the blower and in two minutes my Jeeves was walking down the gravel drive from the main entrance. When he saw me, he waved impatiently to the guard who poked at a button inside his booth. It took him five boozy tries to hit it, and Jeeves was nearly to the gate when a bell finally rang and the gates slowly ground open.

"What is it, Mr. Banyon?" Jeeves demanded, tugging at his cuffs impatiently. "If you're looking for a bonus for this afternoon, you were more than handsomely compensated for a few hours work."

"Yeah, how are my few hours of work feeling?" I droned.

"Ah," Jeeves said, eyes hooded. "The Queen is resting after her ordeal. It was a terrible business, that. Still, accidents happen."

"Yeah, that's why I'm here," I said. "What happened back there wasn't an accident. I'm not sure if they've updated the lingo since I was on the police force, but when I was a cop that's what we used to call a 'premeditated on-purpose.'"

Jeeves turned his head slightly to one side, as if he could get a better grasp of my meaning with his gaze faintly askew. "I beg your pardon?"

"That flying buttress didn't fly on its own. The cops are investigating it now."

"I know that, Mr. Banyon," Jeeves sniffed in reply. "I spoke to the lead officer minutes ago. He assured me that there was no foul play involved."

"Look, I'm not going to say Detective Dan Jenkins is the worst cop in the country. I don't have to. Not after they gave him that award last year in San Diego. But even he's not stupid enough to ignore the forensics report. Give him a couple of days and he'll be back on the phone telling you what I'm telling you now. Someone tried to kill the old bird. Beats me if whoever it is will try again, but consider yourself warned."

A sudden mechanical roar sliced through the night and I glanced over next to the embassy building. The yard was illuminated by floodlights. Two groundskeepers had just started up chainsaws and were bearing down on an old, gnarled tree that grew in a tangle of ancient roots in the middle of the lawn. They attacked from either side, two feet up from the base. Sawdust blew like confetti all around the green grass.

I might not be the most observant private dick in town, but there are things even I can't miss.

"That tree wasn't there this afternoon," I said, frowning.

Jeeves' lips got thinner than the unabridged paperback version of *Blood, Guts and Hot Water: 101 Mouth-Watering Meals by Albion's Top 10 Chefs*.

"I'm sure you are mistaken," Jeeves insisted.

"If you want to join the line of people who think that, I hear these days it starts somewhere west of Nebraska, so wear your hiking jodhpurs. But I'm not wrong. That's where half your kitchen staff was preparing the main course not six hours ago. Last time I was here, there was nothing over there but lawn and one royally pissed-off dragon covered in Worcestershire."

I figured it was one of those magic bean deals. Magic crops are great for farmers who have the equipment and manpower to harvest fast enough. Beans, corn, barley and wheat that grow overnight are a real boon to industrial farming. On the other hand, family farmers who try it invariably wind up over-planting, tearing the hell out of tectonic plates and punching holes through the clouds to Giantland. Don't believe Willie Nelson's Farm Aid line of bullshit. He doesn't give a damn about family farms or giant geese crapping gold eggs, he's in it for the overnight pot.

For his part, Jeeves didn't seem to have a clue what to say when I caught him lying about the tree that hadn't been in his front yard that morning.

"Yes," Jeeves said, in the very slow way men have of talking when they've been caught in an obvious untruth and while a brain that isn't up to the task is processing through a list of even worse lies to cover for the first one.

"Yes," Jeeves repeated, as the invisible gears in his brain continued to spin like an out-of-control ballerina whose smoking toes were about to set fire to the stage.

"Yes," Jeeves said a third time, and the light finally switched on.

He had the drunk guard haul me through the gate and dump me on the sidewalk.

"The Albion government thanks you for your service," Jeeves said through the closed and locked gate. He walked back inside the embassy.

I could still see the two guys hacking at the ancient tree with their chainsaws. Not the brightest way to cut down a tree and, frankly, I didn't want to witness what would happen when the two blades met in the middle of the trunk. Not sober, anyway.

Anyway, I'd done my Boy Scout act and delivered the warning. What the Albions did with the information was entirely up to them. I had a hot date with a cold bar stool that had been waiting patiently all day for my warm ass.

As I walked back down the sidewalk, I heard the tree fatally crack on the far side of the wall. The chainsaws cut to abrupt silence, and I heard the massive crash of the old, gnarled tree as it hit the ground and, judging by the chorus of car alarms that suddenly screamed to life, about twenty royal limos. How these people conquered the world with fifty wooden boats and no toothpaste, I'd never know.

Chapter 5

Drunk philosophers marinating at the end of a bar and crummy pulp writers looking to pad a word count are always talking about the pulse of the city. I don't go in for sappy hokum. If this city had a pulse it was a dying one.

After the day's last commuter had fled to safety behind the locked garage door gates of his mortgaged-to-the-eyeballs suburban castle, the quiet evening took hold of the decaying brownstones and potholed streets like a serial killer softly strangling but never quite murdering the same victim over and over every night. The city's pulse was the barely registering thump in the scrawny chest of the career wino dying in a plastic chair at the free clinic over in Samson Square or the middle-aged whore in some fleabag hotel on Eighth with a needle in her arm and junk coursing through her neon-blue veins. It was the unicorn with the broken horn dying of hepatitis in an empty above-ground pool cage in the worst petting zoo in the world over in the hat factory parking lot or the broke trolls turning tricks for summer squash under the abandoned stockyard bridge.

I wasn't a romantic, a fact that Doris, my ex-wife, and a thousand other floozies would swear to on a stack of bibles. I knew there wasn't a pulse to the city. That conjured an image of a lone being with a single purpose. The jumble through which we all aimlessly staggered was more like four million random dice dumped out on a grimy Monopoly board. Sometimes you hit somebody else's dice, sometimes their dice hit you.

As I walked along the cracked sidewalk that night, I got the distinct feeling that I was about to get slammed in the kisser by someone else's dice, and hard.

The city might not be a living thing, but I'd lived in it long enough to get the gut sense when something was out of place.

I was two blocks from O'Hale's. A punk in his early twenties was making out with a girl centaur in the doorway of a crummy tumbledown apartment building, but other than that the street was empty. When the pair clip-clopped inside the building to get down to the serious work of making their first ugly, six-footed baby, I was alone.

Not a single shadow moved in any of the dimly lit doorways I passed, and not a single living soul walked the silent sidewalk up ahead. I was the last living man on earth...until a minute later when I heard shuffling footfalls.

The soft sound came from somewhere down the vacant street at my back.

I'm not the twitchy type. A guy in my line of work makes more enemies than friends, and if I spent all day looking over my shoulder for everybody who's got it in for me I'd wind up stepping off a blind curb in front of one of those galloping chariots from Ben Hur's House of Pizza. But when my old cop's gut starts screaming out a five alarm warning that I'm about to get my skull cracked in, I know enough to listen.

I glanced back.

At first I didn't see a thing. When I finally did spot the figure slowly shambling along on the other side of the street, I figured that my cop's gut was on the fritz, most likely due to a dangerous lack of the revitalizing lubricant

Ed Jaublowski dispensed from pretty brown bottles behind the bar at O'Hale's.

The figure was small, no more than five feet tall. As it walked, it hung close to the dirty windows and smog-stained walls at the far edge of the sidewalk.

I didn't bolt. I'm smart enough to run like hell from most fights, but this had turned out to be nothing but jittery nerves. I don't break out in a cold sweat because of some midget grammar school kid all alone and out for an evening stroll. Still, there was something off about him. I couldn't see his face, so for all I knew he was staring at his own feet as he shambled along. Even so, I got the sense I was on his radar. I kept an eye on the kid as we both continued down the block.

The doors to each storefront were recessed and the front panes angled in to meet them. At each doorway, the angled glass gave a perfect reflected view of the sidewalk across the street. I'd lose him once I'd passed the doors, but pick him up again at the next one. In the blank spots in between doorways, I kept track of his footfalls.

There were a dozen doors he could have turned in, but he kept walking with that same deliberate shuffle. He stayed on his side of the street for half a block. If he was a mugger wannabe, he was in for a big surprise. TV might have given him other ideas, but not every middle-aged mook in a trench coat is a metrosexual pushover.

I decided to give him a little test. I slowed down. So did he. I picked my pace back up and he sped up right along with me.

Okay, so he was following me. His mistake.

I was coming up on another angled sheet of glass and I suddenly realized that I hadn't heard his last couple of footsteps. They might have been drowned out by the sudden whoosh of an air conditioner unit in one of the apartments above my head, but when I took a look for his reflection I found the kid was gone.

I spun around and realized that he hadn't disappeared completely. He was no longer skulking along the sidewalk on the other side of the street, he was standing right behind me, not ten feet away. The kid was fast, I had to give him that.

I still couldn't see his face. He was wearing a hood, pulled up far and forward so that his face was nothing but a black abyss. He stood just outside the splash of harsh light cast by a flickering, failing streetlight, so I couldn't see the rest of him.

Not that the rest of him mattered. I'd seen enough.

Molokai said that whoever had blackmailed him into attacking the Queen had worn a hood. This thought had scarcely enough time to flit through my brain before the kid leaned over and grabbed a Pathfinder in both hands. One hand pressed under the SUV's bumper, the other clamped down on the hood. When the kid straightened back up, all four tires achieved liftoff and the whole car came right along with him.

With the Pathfinder sticking straight up above him, he looked like a golf tee with a basketball parked on top of it. The car alarm was whooping like every boardwalk Missile Command arcade game going off simultaneously, and the antitheft lights performed a crazy sympathetic disco strobe show.

He stood there for a moment with the Pathfinder held above his head.

Then he threw it at me.

The SUV came flying in like a low-level rocket fired at point blank range. The impact would have crushed every one of my bones like a bag of stomped-on dog biscuits. Beats me how I managed to dive out of its path. I just knew that as tons of Nissan came screaming through the empty air straight at me, I was flinging myself headfirst into the doorway of the nearest closed business.

The car missed me by inches. The hood caught the window on one side of the door, shattering it into a million sparkling shards. It passed over the empty space in front of the recessed doorway and zoomed straight into the window on the far side. It took that one out too, and the Pathfinder kept on going down the street. From the spot where I was flattened on my belly on the store's dirty welcome mat, I heard the flung SUV crashing to crushed bits as it rolled off down the street.

I scrambled to my feet. Glass shards slipped from the back of my trench coat and scattered around my Florsheims. Only then did I realize where I'd taken cover.

I'd done business at Polly Skidmore's Pawn Shop a bunch of times, usually for the kind of high-end electronic gizmos that come in handy in my profession. Polly sold or rented cheap, but it didn't look like I'd be doing much business there for a little while.

The front of Polly Skidmore's was suddenly Christmas morning to neighborhood looters. Both front windows were gone, panes shattered and frames snapped. A couple of big-screen plasma TVs had been wiped out and handfuls of voodoo dolls and cheap costume jewelry had spilled onto the sidewalk for the taking.

I crushed some Mardi Gras beads underfoot as I stuffed my hand under my armpit where my gat nestled in its holster in the warm spot under my arm. I yanked the gun out and dropped to one knee, peering around the remnants of the front wall.

This time it was Subaru. The figure in the hood was holding a blue Outback over one shoulder and waiting patiently for me to pop my head up like a gopher. When I did, he let the next car fly.

I played a little football back in school a million years ago. Baseball was never my game. Don't put a bat in my hand if I can't crack somebody's head open with it. But at that moment I knew what they meant about seeing the stitches on a fastball.

The Subaru was coming in at a downward angle and heading straight at the front of Polly Skidmore's. Another second and it'd sweep me up and carry me straight back into the store, a pulverized P.I. in a blood-spattered trench coat.

The car spun in the air, like the slow-motion instant replay of the last seconds of a pathetic life poorly lived. I saw passenger door, roof, driver's door. It whistled as it spun. I noticed the ding in the front panel near the bumper and wondered if it came from a grocery store shopping cart a month ago or from the punk kid who'd just flung it at me. Only one way to find out. I'd have to ask him.

I jumped from behind the remnants of the pawn shop wall and ran straight at the flying car. At the last second, I dropped to the sidewalk and rolled. The Subaru passed straight over me like the shadow of death. An instant later it punched through what was left of the front of Polly Skidmore's Pawn Shop and kept right on going, vanishing deep inside the store. The burglar alarm abruptly howled to life and I barely had time to wonder what the hell kind of outfit Polly was running that the alarm didn't go off when somebody smashes out both front windows.

The kid was shuffling down the street. No hurry with this guy.

I saw now in the stark light of a better streetlamp that his hooded sweatshirt was bulky, and that he was round at the middle; sort of bell-shaped. He was wearing matching black sweatpants and the littlest sneakers I've ever seen on a boy.

"This have anything to do with me personally or are these just random acts of violence? Because I'll be more than happy to tag in another pedestrian to take my place in the ring. You ever hear of a cop named Jenkins?"

The hooded figure reached out for a parked BMW.

"Oh, it's a foreign car thing," I said. "Hey, I'd be swingin' away right there with you, pal, if Detroit didn't make shitboxes for cars these days. I'd ride my toaster to work before I got in one of those Chevy Volts. Although on the plus side, even I can pick up one of those hunks of hippie junk. Not that that's all that impressive. You can crush a Volt on your forehead like an empty beer can."

He didn't even look at me. He grabbed the BMW by the nose and began to lift.

I cocked the hammer on my roscoe. "Don't, kid," I warned.

I didn't know what he was. He obviously wasn't human. I didn't even know what gender he was any longer. It was simpler to think that someone flinging cars at me like Frisbees was male, but it might not be the case. A few years back I was hired by the Women's Tennis Association to check out a new heavy-hitter with a powerhouse serve who was beating all the other gals on the tour. A simple background check turned up her real name. The chick was Hermaphroditus, and she was the son of some ancient gods. Greeks, I think. Birth certificate was impossible to get since it was wiped out when Atlantis General Hospital sank in some earthquake; but I did get a copy of her driver's license from DMV, plus an old library card and Discover credit card info. She'd been born a guy, fused with a water nymph to became a he/she, apparently laid low for a few thousand years, then turned up running a scam on the ladies tennis circuit. I solved that one fast, but never took the cash or told the clients the truth. Hey, call me a bleeding heart all you want, but if they didn't ban Martina Navratilova for being a shaved sasquatch, they had no right to dump some half-man-god-nymph-thing. Guy still sends me a box of baklava as a thank-you every Christmas.

On the street outside the shattered storefront of Polly Skidmore's Pawn Shop, the figure in the hood held the BMW at chest level and peered around the car's trunk at the handgun I had leveled on its chest.

I still couldn't see its face, but it seemed to be taking a long, hard look. Staring down the barrel of a heater has a tendency to put the least introspective individual into a contemplative frame of mind.

I knew I was shit out of luck when the hood of the Beemer collapsed in a V shape under his hand like he was folding laundry. He brought the car up over his shoulder, but I wasn't giving him his third swing at bat.

I sent two slugs screaming from the barrel of my automatic.

I didn't miss. I'm a lot of things, most of them bad, but one thing I'm not is a lousy shot. The bullets thumped into his chest, but they didn't slow him down. He didn't even shrug them off. They were nothing to him. No effect at all.

There are plenty of tough guys out there who can shake off a couple of point-blank rounds. Bullets are less than mosquito bites to zombies, and I've known vampires who try not to flinch when you're blowing holes through their lungs, but that's usually to impress undead groupies.

I once saw a guy empty a clip into an ogre who didn't drop his club, but the autopsy afterwards showed the thing was high on Dutch Cleanser.

The fact is, even the creatures that can take a few rounds without going down for the count show some reaction to getting shot, even if it's just a pointed grunt to tell you how pissed off you've made them as they try to peel your eyes like grapes. But with my pal in the hooded sweatshirt it was 1.) get shot, 2.) car up and business as usual.

Lucky for me he took a second to wind up. Discretion is the better part of valor, and running away is the best part of not getting a couple of tons of precision Nazi auto engineering planted between your ears. I turned and flew like hell down the alley next to Polly Skidmore's Pawn Shop.

More luck for me, he couldn't plant the square peg in the square hole. The car could've slipped right up the alley if he'd managed to get it through nose-first. Instead, it slammed in broadside and got wedged in the mouth of the alley. A tire wrenched off and bounced right at me. I had to flatten hard against the wall as it bounced past.

My hooded pal started pounding on the far side of the wedged BMW. The frame bent and the engine block dropped out like a horse I'd seen giving birth on TV the previous week when I was too drunk to change the channel. (Goddamn National Geographic Channel.)

Over the pounding on the car was the sound of Polly's burglar alarm on the other side of the wall against which my back was plastered. And over the staccato *ahn-ahn* whine of the alarm I was never happier to hear the shriek of a police cruiser.

Bricks tore lose at the corners of both buildings against which the Beemer was wedged. They broke to pieces on the alley floor amid clouds of mortar dust.

I was in a dead end. The alley stopped at a sheer brick wall, there were no doors or windows, and the only fire escape was too high for me to grab. The only way out was the way I came in, and the car that blocked the mouth of the alley continued to bend slowly inward with each echoing punch the punk gave the roof on the other side.

The cop car finally broke into the block outside Polly Skidmore's and I heard it squeal to a stop somewhere near the pawn shop. I could see over the twisted BMW the flashing red and blue lights playing a crazy kaleidoscopic dance all over the walls and windows of the tenements across the street.

"Freeze!" an unseen cop yelled.

Things suddenly got a whole lot crazier, and from the crashing, the shouting, the gunfire, and the fact that the cruiser lights abruptly snapped out, I figured the cops had been treated to an encore performance of my buddy's amazing one-man car juggling act.

The gunplay grew muffled and I knew the cops had chased the hooded figure into the pawn shop. I heard glass shattering somewhere past the walled-up end of the alley and a sudden air conditioner whoosh like I'd heard out front. This time it was louder, and this time I knew it didn't come from any beat-up old Kenmore X-tra Kool Deluxe hanging from the window of a rat-infested walkup apartment.

The whoosh became a roar and something bright streaked across the night sky.

It traveled in an arc, like a shooting star thrown into reverse. The yellow streak disappeared almost as quickly as it had flashed to life. The whooshing sound faded in the distance and all that remained for noise was the burglar alarm, the cops yelling in back of Polly Skidmore's Pawn Shop, and the blood pounding a symphony in my own ears.

In all the excitement, I'd forgotten about the four grand in my pocket. It could have fallen out anywhere. I quickly patted my chest and felt the comfortable lump of the fat envelope beneath my coat.

The blood symphony stopped playing bongos and cymbals in my head and I heaved a sigh of relief. Hey, mayhem and death I can deal with, but I've got a growing liver and a couple of dependent kidneys to worry about.

I stuffed my gat back in my holster, walked over to the blocked mouth of the alley and began the pain in the ass climb up the undercarriage of the wrecked BMW.

Chapter 6

"I ought to toss you in the drunk tank for public brawling."

"I'm not drunk, Jenkins, I only wish I was. The pamphlets they pass out to tourists at the bus station say it's the only way to get through an interview with you."

Just my luck, Detective Daniel Jenkins was the ranking cop on duty.

I hadn't been arrested, but I'd been hauled in for questioning.

The two cops whose cruiser had been flattened by a flying Passat were looking none too happy as they filled out paperwork in the squad room outside Jenkins' office.

The owners of two of the four cars that had been demolished had arrived on the scene minutes after the cops chased off my hooded attacker. A cruiser had been sent off to track down the missing owners of the BMW and the Subaru.

Polly Skidmore had shown up in person to shut off the burglar alarm. Polly was an eight hundred pound sack of hairy meat in a dirty, stretched wife-beater T-shirt and a pair of trademark busting-apart plaid pants that had been blocked from his personal bird's eye view by an acre of belly fat since about when Carter was in the White House.

I caught a break with Polly. He was so mad at the cops for chasing their fugitive straight through the back wall of his pawn shop that he was laying all the blame on the city's finest. Guy was screaming so hard when he saw the car parked in the middle of his store that I thought he'd stroke out right then and there. As it was, they had to pull one of his own voodoo dolls from his fat hands, but not before one of the cops outside had his appendix ruptured by the pin Polly jabbed into the doll's belly. He was being booked downstairs for, among other charges, redirected assault on a police officer with a deadly simulacrum.

I was hoping in all the excitement that I'd get dropped through the stationhouse cracks, but Jenkins was being his usual darling self.

"How did you provoke him, Banyon?" the flatfoot demanded.

"I didn't provoke anyone," I insisted.

"You're provoking *me*," Jenkins sneered.

"In that case, next time your goons haul me in for no reason I promise not to wear my low-cut holster."

I could see I was burrowing under his skin like a tick in a Tijuana whorehouse.

"You've got a smart answer for everything, don't you, Banyon?" he fumed.

"Just keeping the scales in balance with all the stupid questions you're asking, Detective Jenkins." I jumped in before he could get out another hollow bread-and-water threat. "I told you, I was attacked."

"Says you. And for no reason whatsoever."

"Oh, there was a reason," I said. "I just don't know what it is yet."

"And whoever it was conveniently avoided two city cops, busted straight through the back of that pawn shop and took off like a rocket?"

"Hey, your cops saw the same thing as me, Jenkins. He must've had one of those Japanese jetpacks stashed behind Polly's like they used to fly the new emperor out when that giant moth attacked New Tokyo last month. Personally, I believe if God had meant for man to fly He wouldn't have put all the distilleries down here."

Jenkins tapped the chewed stub of an eraser on his #2 pencil on the scarred surface of his old desk. He could usually go for hours busting my chops, but that night he looked too worn out to play. I figured I knew the reason why.

"I take it forensics explained to you that granite doesn't fall sideways," I said.

The cop's mug soured. "Oh, you're not so smart. I know somebody threw that butter-tress at the Queen," Jenkins said, flinging his pencil at a pile of paperwork on the corner of his desk. "It's not like you've got the only set of eyes in town, Banyon. I saw it as soon as you left just by looking over the side of the church."

If he thought I believed that whopper, I figured I could sell him a rainbow bridge to ferret heaven, but I didn't feel like dealing with the bunco squad once he found out he'd been ripped off. Besides, I already had a load of spending money burning a hole in my pocket and closing time was closing in. I just wanted out of there.

"So you know somebody tried to murder the Queen. Good for you, Jenkins. Did they figure out for you why someone scratched out everything but 'veritas?'"

"That Latin on the wall? St. Regent's is an old church. That's probably been scratched up like that for years."

He spoke with the supreme confidence of a complete moron.

"Right. And those fresh granite chips underneath were just gargoyle spoor. Jenkins, it'd be obvious to a ten year old with a Dick Tracy two-way wrist radio that somebody thinks he knows the truth about something."

No one pulls a look of blank incomprehension like Dan Jenkins, Ace Detective.

"Veritas," I explained. "*Truth* in Latin? Listen, just have somebody look it up for you, Jenkins. You're trying so hard to get it that you look like you're going to trip all the circuits on the board. I'd guess whoever it was is threatening to spill this secret truth, whatever it is, and that 'veritas' is a warning. Think blackmail."

"You've seen too many movies, Banyon," Jenkins said.

Let someone else figure it out for him. I wasn't about to do all his work for him.

"At least you know now the Queen's in danger," I said. "You can bump up security for her appearance with the mayor at city hall tomorrow."

"I know what you're angling for, Banyon, and you're not getting anywhere near this one. If someone's going to murder the Queen, they're going to do it while professional police officers are guarding her. The last thing the chief wants is some hot-dogging P.I. hogging all the glory on the nightly news again."

"What do you mean again?" I asked.

His lips puckered like a dame who'd just had a pair of eight pound lemon collagen injections. "You know what I mean," he said. "It's been all over the news all night, you running across that stage and grabbing the Queen. Nobody likes a glory hound, Banyon."

I didn't tell him that I hadn't been anywhere near a TV all night, other than the plasma screens in Polly Skidmore's display window, and those had been turned off even before a flying Pathfinder's bumper had voided the warranties.

So, someone in a hood arranged for the Queen of Albion to get attacked, I wound up on TV saving her life, and a few hours later I was in the crosshairs of a guy in a hood. P.I. school would be nothing but hygiene films and field trips to the Famous Fingerprints Museum if every case was as easy to follow as this one.

"I talked to the Albions, and they're not going with outside help next time," Jenkins said. "I don't even know why they hired you this time. When they came to me at the last minute looking for a P.I. to work security, I told them to steer clear of you."

"Who came to you?" I asked.

Jenkins snarled. "I don't have to answer your questions, Banyon."

I could play the game too. Besides, I'd had it up to here with Dan Jenkins. I got to my feet. "Unless you plan on booking the hero who saved the Queen of Albion for the crime of nearly being killed, I'm taking my ball and going home."

The fight drained from his shoulders. Jenkins grunted.

"Don't leave town," he warned.

If there'd been a travel agent standing in the corner of his office I would have booked a flight to Tahiti right then and there out of pure malice. Too bad there was only a coat rack. I grabbed my trench coat and fedora and headed out the door.

"Yeah, it's a regular P.I. holiday around here today," Jenkins called after me. "First Harvey Smook, then you. At least he was easier to process through than you."

Harvey Smook was technically a P.I. He'd passed the test and got the license. But none of the rest of us in the pathetic fraternity took the poor slob seriously. I was surprised Smook had registered as more than a speck of dust on the radar screen of the metropolitan police.

I turned back to the smug flatfoot sitting behind the same beat-up old desk where he'd probably have his first five heart attacks. "Why, what did Smook do?" I asked.

"What he did he didn't do neat, that's for sure," Jenkins scoffed. "Made a real mess for Doc Minto to sponge up. They've got him in a couple of buckets downstairs, if you want to pay your last respects."

Jenkins snatched his pencil back up and began furiously ignoring me as he scribbled notes in a yellow legal pad. I noted the chickens, fish and a giraffe he'd doodled in the margins. There was no doubt about it. If the Albions were betting all their moolah that this particular great detective would figure out who was behind these attacks, by the time they got back home to Europe they'd be broker than one of my Saturday night promises come Sunday morning, plus they'd be able to slip what was left of their Queen under the front door of Monmouth Palace.

"If you're a good boy, Jenkins, I'll have the sergeant downstairs send up some finger paints and a carton of chocolate milk."

I turned my back to him and so I only heard the tip of the pencil snap under the pressure. With all the weight the world was putting on that spluttering brain it was only a matter of time before Dan Jenkins would snap next.

Chapter 7

I stopped in at the morgue on my way out of the police station.

Doc Minto, the ancient M.E. who'd run the joint forever, had left for the night and there was only an attendant on duty. The doc was a good guy and probably would have spilled the beans on what happened with Harvey Smook. I didn't have a clue if the kid who showed me the body was a good guy, but he did spill his lunch when he got a good look at the big plate of spaghetti and squashed meatballs that had been Harvey Smook.

Smook the Schnook was what we in the profession called him. It was way too obvious and far too accurate to pass up. Taking a look at the Schnook's scrambled remains lying in a couple of pans in that morgue drawer, I felt kind of guilty for coining then popularizing the nickname at every opportunity. (Yeah, well, he wasn't a platter of pâté when I came up with it. Sue me for being a master of observational humor.)

I took a look at the Schnook's chart, but Doc Minto could teach a medical school course in lousy handwriting. The police report was pinned below. According to the cops, Harvey Smook had climbed to the top of a building over on Lexington, the same block his office was on, and threw himself off the roof. No sweat for a pigeon, but spectacularly fatal for a five foot, four inch butterball P.I. with adenoids.

"I'll dedicate the first half of tonight's bender to you, Schnook," I said.

The second half would be in memory of the sorry street sweeper who'd got stuck scraping up whatever was left glued to the pavement after the cops had finished bagging and tagging the biggest chunks that had exploded out of the busted bag of Schnook.

#

I took the back entrance from the morgue to the parking garage behind Main Police H.Q., Precinct #1. The odds were good somebody was gunning for me, and I wasn't about to deliver myself gift-wrapped to them by marching out the front door. I much prefer taking somebody else's life in my hands than my own.

The streets were quiet so late at night, and for a nice change of pace no one was tossing cars at me.

The crowd at O'Hale's Bar was thinner than I expected. I'd been so eager to get out of the station once I'd left Harvey Schnook to puddle in peace that I hadn't bothered to check the time. It turned out there were so few people at my favorite watering hole because I'd been hanging around the precinct house until the middle of the night. Add one more entry to the list of a million and one reasons to hate Dan Jenkins.

The barkeep, Ed Jaublowski, was looking fat and haggard and all-around ugly, so at least that was business as usual.

"Pour me whatever paint thinner is closest, Ed, and keep refilling," I said as I slid onto my favorite stool. "A dry glass means I am too, and sobriety is the peasant's path through life. You can hang that over the urinal, no charge."

Ed glanced at the clock on the wall, harrumphed, then filled a tumbler.

"I seen you on the news," the barkeep said.

One of the local channels reruns the eleven o'clock news in the wee hours. It came on the set above the bar five minutes later.

I was the top news story, although you wouldn't know it from what you could see. The cameras were aimed at the Queen, and I was just some nobody in a trench coat running across the stage and scooping her up from behind the podium.

The granite chunk of cathedral dropped in much faster than I remembered. Real life was far less scary than the replay. That afternoon it seemed like I had all the time in the world to tap dance across the stage. On video, I'd barely gotten the Queen out of there before the huge blur dropped into frame and the podium along with a large piece of the stage went instantly bye-bye. They reran it in slow-mo a couple of times, but actually seeing every fine crack in the surface of the flying buttress as it pulverized the podium where I'd been standing a second before made me feel like getting down on all fours and kissing the filthy barroom floor. I owed Molokai a sock on his pretty demon jaw.

"How'd you know it was me?" I asked Ed.

Jaublowski was leaning a hairy elbow on the bar and watching his best customer on TV. At least what he could see of me up there. My back was to the camera, and even in slow motion you couldn't get a good look at my face.

"C'mon, Jinx," Jaublowski said. "You got any idea how many times I thrown that moldy coat of yours in your face when I shoved you outta here?"

The reporter hadn't even said my name. Just that I was somebody working security at the event.

"At least I caught one lucky break in a fantastically lousy day," I said as I took a pull on the brown shoe polish Ed had just dumped in my glass.

"Mmm," Jaublowski grunted, not listening any longer. He was busy trying to pry open the crooked cash register drawer. Two paying customers had just stepped up to the bar, and patrons with money always took precedence over me, even creeps like these.

The dame was a Yahoo. You don't see many of them around town, but I was pretty sure this one had moved into a sewer pipe by the chemical plant on Twelfth. I'd seen her crawling in and out of it a bunch of times carting leftovers from the Subway Dumpster. A couple of times I'd spotted her digging for grubs in the vacant lot around the corner from O'Hale's. She had a real chip on her shoulder to go along with all the wriggling maggots, and it was clear she was itching for somebody in O'Hale's to complain about her and her date, a sloppy drunk Oompa-Loompa half her age. But O'Hale's wasn't the Ritz and even freaks like her could count on the same lousy service and watered-down booze as everybody else. Jaublowski was just in it for the dough which, once he got the register drawer to open, he grabbed from the Oompa-Loompa's tiny little orange hand and stuffed away for safe keeping.

I think the Yahoo chick thought her stench was going to at least chase me down to the next stool, but if O'Hale's rat and chupacabra infestations of a couple of summers back didn't get me to budge my ass, what chance did she have?

The two of them staggered to the door. The guy had out a set of miniature car keys. He must've belonged to the blueberry golf cart I'd seen on the way in. I was glad I wasn't walking home any time soon. Some drunk Oompa slams into you full speed in one of those things, you're nursing a bruised ankle for a whole damn week.

The lady Yahoo grabbed the doorframe for support and swung back around to face the bar. "Yeah, youse all a buncha bums!" she yelled at the nearly empty barroom before she stumbled out after her midget boyfriend.

She was filthy, yeah, but perceptive.

"You see me on any of the other channels?" I asked Jaublowski once it was down to just me and him at the bar. Only a couple more losers loitered in the booths. The barkeep shook his head. "I only seen one other, and it was the same angle. I think they used -- what do they call it -- a pool camera?"

I nodded that he'd got it right. One camera, one angle, which meant no shot of my face on screen. Jenkins was peeved for nothing.

I figured when Detective Jackass Jenkins told me I'd made the news that I'd be swamped with calls from every sobbing housewife with a cheating husband looking for the famous private eye who'd saved Her Royal Pocketbook. At least now I knew that me and the serious hangover I planned to be nursing the next morning wouldn't have to deal with a ringing phone and a nuisance parade of paying clients all day.

More good news. The day that ended at midnight might've been for crap, and I was sure from years of experience that tomorrow would turn out lousy too, but at that moment I was nestled smack-dab in the middle of one of those rare meteorological golden moments between the two fronts of competing shit storms.

"You ever hear of a schmuck name of Harvey Smook?" I asked Jaublowski.

The barkeep was keeping an eye aimed at the wall and not my glass as he poured me another. He shook his head while pouring blind and didn't spill a drop.

"He's in the book," I said, "but he won't be in the next one. Here's to you, Schnook." I pounded down the brown bleach in one gulp and slammed the tumbler back to the bar. This time, for some deeply troubling reason, it remained empty.

Jaublowski was returning the bottle to the shelf behind the bar.

"Let me empty one before you start me on another," I said.

"Sorry, Jinx," Jaublowski said. "Closing time."

Ed Jaublowski was one Polish joke I never got.

"What the hell are you talking about?" I asked.

"Cops have been all over all the bars around town," Ed said. "Temperance League is putting the screws to all of us ever since those kids busted into the high school and trashed the place. Ain't you seen it in the paper?"

"Paperboy wised up and stopped delivering it when I didn't pay him for six weeks. Are you serious?"

He was, but looked none too happy about it. "Little shits get loaded and let a griffin loose on the brand new gym floor, and I gotta pay the penalty. It ain't fair, Jinx."

I could tell him a thing or two about fair, especially after the day I'd had. It takes time to work up a good head of drunk, especially when you've built up as much immunity as I have, and what I'd polished off so far was more like a flu shot. It'd take one hell of a lot more than a couple of belts for the full-blown, fun-filled influenza effect, with accompanying headache, nausea, chills, and Technicolor vomiting.

"C'mon, Ed, be a human being for once, will you? I wasted the whole day not getting drunk." I nudged the glass in his direction, but Jaublowski didn't budge. He glanced at two quiet bums slouching in a corner booth like they might be undercover agents for the tea-totaling Gestapo.

"No can do, Jinx," he insisted.

I reached into the envelope in my pocket and slapped a dub onto the bar. "Just gimme one of those for the road," I snarled, waving at the bottles lined up at the back of the bar. "And make sure it's not one of your watered down specials. I want to start a fire, not put one out."

Jaublowski showed me his watch. "Can't do it. It's after two."

I'd seen Ed Jaublowski peddling hooch to high school kids at six in the morning. On prom night, there were so many limos lined up around the block that O'Hare's looked like the Kodak Theatre on Oscar night.

I grabbed my twenty off the bar and jammed it back in my pocket. I didn't say another word to the traitor Jaublowski, and he was so embarrassed to be turning me out on the street with the rest of the riffraff stragglers from his corner booths that he didn't even grouse that I hadn't paid him for the couple of drinks he'd poured down me.

With the door to O'Hare's locked at my back and no liquor stores open so late at night, I had no entertainment options left open to me.

There might have been something left in a stray bottle back at my apartment, but the long walk would be too much to bear if I got there and that wound up being a bust too. My office was closer. Thanks to the tippling mice living in the walls it was dry as a Seventh-day Adventist St. Patrick's Day bacchanal, but the couch worked double duty as a bed, and now that I was already wading hip-deep into the excremental joy of a new day I just wanted to pull up the covers and see if sleep alone could accomplish that for which alcohol was the accepted prescribed cure by ten out of ten drunks.

When I trudged up to my building the first thing I saw was that despite the late hour there was a light on in my office. The second thing I could spy from the street below was a very large shadow playing off the walls and ceiling.

My first instinct was to walk right on by and slog home to my apartment, but pigheaded curiosity won out. I needed to find out if my bastard pal in the hood had come back with a Miata tucked under his arm to finish the job.

I'm not big on storming the beach. You're more likely to find me in a beach-adjacent tavern nursing a bad sunburn and a bottle of Bacardi. With self-preservation utmost in my mind, I eschewed the front door in favor of the fire escape.

I slipped my piece from its holster but wasn't as reassured as I normally am by its weight in my palm as I climbed up to the window with my name painted on it.

The giant shadow on the ceiling turned out to be cast by a small elf crouching in front of an upended lamp.

I tapped the barrel of my gat on the window, and Mannix looked up with a start. When he saw it was me, he hustled over to unlatch the window.

"Mr. Crag!" the elf exclaimed. "You're all right."

"That remains to be seen, kid," I replied as I climbed into the office. "What the hell happened here?"

Mannix had been pawing at paperwork on the linoleum beside my desk. My file cabinet had been upended and all my case files were dumped out on the floor. It looked as if Mannix was trying to sort the scraps of paper back into the proper manila folders.

My desk was shoved a few inches back, like someone had tried to tip it over too, only to realize it was so weighed down by junk in the drawers that all it could do was scrape a couple of black stripes across the cheap floor. When they'd failed to knock over my desk, they'd swept the stuff on the surface to the floor. Most of it was still down there, although Mannix had replaced the phone and the copy of the book Merlin had given me, which he must have retrieved from the closet floor after I'd left that morning.

My coat rack over by the door had been shoved over and one of the eight hooks had snapped off. No big loss, since I only ever used two. I straightened up the rack and decorated my favorite two hooks with my coat and hat as Mannix bounded alongside me.

"He was very angry," the elf explained. "He burst in after you were on the news yesterday evening and started throwing things around. It was very naughty of him to do this to someone else's things. He did all this and then he--" Mannix threw up his helpless little hands and exhaled. "--well, he just left. I've been trying to get your files back in order all day long, but Miss Doris' system is very confusing."

"Doris and the alphabet aren't on speaking terms," I explained. "She takes a Zen approach to filing, which to the layman's eye looks a lot like shoving paperwork inside the nearest convenient file and slamming the drawer shut while screaming at me for her grievance du jour. So this guy who trashed the office. Was he just over five feet tall, wearing a hood and carrying a Volkswagen in his pocket?"

Mannix shook his head vigorously. "He was..." The elf hustled over to the desk and snatched up a business card from the corner. "He was him."

I looked at the card. Three colors. Fat lot of good the fancy, multicolored embossed business card had done him. In the middle of the card was neatly printed:

HARVEY SMOOK
PRIVATE INVESTIGATOR

"Oh, damn. When was Smook here?"

"I told you, after you were on the news. I remember I'd just watched you save the nice lady in the blue dress. I was watching it live, just as it happened." Mannix pulled a very somber frown. "I'm sorry that they didn't show your face or give your name, Mr. Crag. That was very mean of them to not tell everyone that you did such a nice thing."

"Yeah, it's a national tragedy, Mannix. I'm leading a march on Washington the minute I get my good argyle protest socks back from the cleaners. What about Smook?"

"Oh," the elf said. "Well, he came limping in about twenty minutes after that and started throwing things around and yelling that you stole his big break. When I told him that you were good and not naughty and that you most definitely did not steal things, he threw his business card at me, told me to tell you that you were going to get yours and that it didn't matter what you'd done to get on TV, and that he was going to bust the case wide open. Then he limped out on his crutches and slammed the door. He was a very bad man."

"No, Mannix," I said, shaking my head. "Harvey Smook wasn't a bad guy. He was a loser, definitely a sad sack, but he wasn't bad. This isn't like him." I nodded to the mess he'd made of the office. "You sure it was Smook? Short, fat, Coke-bottle glasses? What about the whine? Did his voice sound like somebody'd shoved a weed whacker and a bunch of mosquitoes up both nostrils?"

At each physical trait, Mannix nodded more vigorously. So it *was* Smook the Schnook who'd barged into my office and made a mess of the place.

I kicked my desk back to a reasonable approximation of where it had been moored for the past decade and dropped into my chair.

This was just perfect. There was now a direct link from the oozing remains of Harvey Smook over at the morgue back to me: the Schnook himself.

"Do you know why he was on crutches?" I asked.

"He had a cast on his leg," Mannix said. "This leg." He pointed at his right leg and offered a helpful smile.

A thought immediately sprang to mind, but I chalked it up to the late hour and the side effects of an unpolluted blood stream. The world was nuts, but it wasn't that nuts.

I could definitely use a belt but thanks to the mice snoring off their bender in the walls, mine was now a dry office. It was late. I was tired.

"Go home, Mannix. Get some shut-eye."

"Yes, sir, Mr. Crag."

I stopped him before he could hustle halfway to the door. "Wait," I said, fishing in my wallet. I passed him a fin. "Here. Run out and pick me up a paper on your way in tomorrow. I've got a hostile letter to write to the editor, and I want to know exactly who in the Temperance League deserves the biggest up-yours."

The elf accepted the bill and hurried from the room, offering a cheery good-night on his way out the door. I heard the outer door shut and the lock click a moment later.

I sat alone and disgustingly sober for a long time, contemplating the past twenty-four hours.

A simple bodyguard gig had almost killed me. A faceless would-be killer on the street had tried playing pin-the-tail-on-the-donkey on my head with a BMW. A fellow P.I. with a well-earned reputation as a milquetoast had gone O.J. on my office, only to wind up a plate of raw hamburger just after leaving my place according to the report I'd seen at the M.E.'s. Dan Jenkins would be spinning like Julie Andrews and belting out a show-stopping number on the stationhouse roof when he got that particular joyous news. There was only one reason for all of it.

"Mondays," I said. "I'm never coming in to work on one again."

Before I went to sleep on the couch, I helped Mannix with the paperwork by gathering up an armload off the floor and filing it in the wastebasket under W.

Chapter 8

I awoke with the sun beating on my face through the open blinds, the radiator in the corner clanking like a rusty suit of armor falling down a flight of stairs, and the barrel of my own gun pointed at my right eyeball.

The mice that had been terrorizing the building had staggered out of their hole in the baseboard while I was asleep. They'd made it up to the sofa cushion where I'd spent a couple of hours drooling onto a souvenir *Jaws* pillow Doris had brought back from a vacation at Universal Studios in California. Two of the little vermin were propping up the barrel of my gun on either side while the third held the trigger with both front paws.

They had the look of desperate drunks on their rodent faces, and the one at the trigger was jerking his head in the direction of the empty booze bottles in the closet.

I was saved from an eye patch over a permanent tunnel through to the back of my head by Mannix, who picked that moment to spring the office door.

The mice panicked and the two holding the gun dropped it. When the third fell, he yanked the trigger and the shark on the pillow sprouted a smoking hole in the middle of his gaping mouth. Lucky for me, I'd already shoved myself up out of the way.

The mice landed on the floor and scattered. One of them dropped onto a toppled-over bottle and raced it to the door of the closet on two desperately pumping hind feet like an expert log-roller.

The first two mice vanished into the closet, the third banged his rolling bottle off the wall and fell off. He jumped up, and when he ran in after the first pair I heard a snap.

"Little bastards," I growled, grabbing and holstering my piece before hustling over to the closet.

The first two had gotten away through a crack in the plaster. The third was lying bug-eyed in the mouse trap that had snapped its neck.

Anthropomorphic mice always wear identical turtlenecks; the only thing different about them is the color. This one's was red. He'd also been wearing a tiny red beret, which had flown off when the trap was sprung.

I'd invested in the traps the previous week, three for a buck at Wal-Mart, but I'd only caught two of the buggers so far. The infestation was far more than a couple of cheap mousetraps could handle.

"What line of bullshit did Johansen feed you?" I asked Mannix as I picked up the trap and walked it over to the overflowing trash bucket.

"Mr. Bob says that an exterminator is coming tomorrow," the elf replied. He was back on the floor he'd abandoned the previous night and was sorting once more through what was left of the paperwork.

"Is that the same tomorrow that slob promised two weeks ago or the one from a month ago? He's sung that goddamn song more than Little Orphan Annie."

I stomped my foot down into the trash barrel, but the paperwork I'd so carefully filed the night before hardly budged. With the trash full, I went with option B. I brought the mouse to the window and let the whole thing -- trap and all -- drop. It landed on a crate of mackerel that was rotting on a pile of ice in front of the first-floor fish market. A dead mouse in a turtleneck lying in a box of steaming fish would only be the worst health code violation at Luigi Vincetti's For the Halibut Fish Bazaar on a very slow day.

When I turned back to my desk, Mannix had somehow laid out the morning paper along with a tidy stack of change from my five dollar bill when I wasn't looking.

The entire first page was dedicated to the Queen. The headline screamed **CHECKMATE!**, and was accompanied by a picture of the flying buttress sticking up from the remains of the stage. Checkers is more my speed, and even I know that in chess you check the king not the queen. Another red letter day for the geniuses of the Fourth Estate.

I scanned all the front page stories. The bulk of the ink had been used up on the attempt on the Queen's life, most of that on the banner headline. There was a story about the Queen's official visit at city hall at noon that day. A side story mentioned that Prince Gormless, her eldest son and heir to the Albion throne, was spending the week crouching in a swamp back home to stop a supermarket from being built. The closest I got to being mentioned in the paper was as an "unidentified private security agent" in the lead story.

I figured as much. The phone had remained blessedly free of pain-in-the-ass would-be clients all night.

The silent phone was good news for another reason. It meant Dan Jenkins hadn't found out that the late Harvey Smook had paid Banyon Investigations a surprise visit the previous day.

Before I fell asleep on my lumpy office sofa, I had wrestled for a total of one soul-wrenching second with the question of whether I should let the cops know about Smook stopping by to say hi before he went splat. I decided that there was no way in hell I was going to waltz in to Precinct #1 and give Jenkins the pleasure of hauling me down to lockup yet again. If he wanted a cheap thrill let him hire a hooker, assuming he could find one whose self-esteem was rock-bottom even by whore standards.

Still, it'd be best if I tried to figure out just why the Schnook was pitching a fit in my office just in case Jenkins came sniffing around.

Info on the latest activities of the meddling Temperance League biddies was only one of the reasons I'd had Mannix pick up the paper. I shook the *Gazette* open to the obituaries. Harvey Smook stared back at me from the top of the page.

Everybody expects a certain amount of flowery horseshit when it comes to obits. You never know when the dearly departed might linger on as a ghost, and nobody wants to risk accurately describing late Uncle Schmendrick as a bow-legged son-of-a-bitch if there's a remote chance he's refused to cross over. If you thought he was a bastard when he was alive, piss him off in his obit and get used to washing ectoplasm out of your shoes on a daily basis and having chains rattling nonstop in your ear for the duration of every hangover for the rest of your life. But even by the relaxed rules of encomium writing, Smook's obituary was embroidered more than Grandma's best company doilies.

"'Top in his field?'" I said. "It took the Schnook three tries to graduate Matchbook Detective School, and they mail out diplomas to dogs. I knew a schnauzer got one by mistake a couple years back who was a better private eye than Harvey Smook. It says here he died 'while working on the case of his career.' If he had a case when he died it would've been the only case of his career since no one was ever stupid or desperate enough to hire Harvey Smook to work a case."

I was ready to toss the paper down to the fish market. I'd already wadded it up when my brain suddenly caught up with something my eye had seen a moment before.

I rapidly unfolded the *Gazette* back to the obituaries and smoothed out the crumpled pages.

The story hadn't been on the obituary page, but on the page adjacent to it.

BODY DISCOVERED IN COUNTY LANDFILL

It wasn't the headline that had caught the attention of my sluggish brain, but the picture that accompanied it. There was a sketch included alongside the story of the poor slob who'd been interred with the city's rotting Pampers and pizza boxes.

I knew the guy. And unlike the usual vagrants I know who wind up dead in the landfill, this one wasn't broke. At least not judging by the four grand worth of ruby he'd dropped on my desk just yesterday morning.

The sketch was of Merlin, Albion's official royal wizard and one of the Queen's advance team. Whoever had killed him had dressed him like a bum in a Dodgers hat before they'd dumped him in the dump. The story also said his feet had been cut off.

I'm a lot of things, but stupid isn't usually one of them. The infernal curse of forced sobriety had dropped my I.Q. into the subbasement.

"Damn."

Mannix, still sorting papers on the floor, glanced up. "Is there something wrong, Mr. Crag?" the elf asked.

"It's the damn mice's fault," I said. "I do my best thinking loaded, and they polished off my office supply. *Merlin* was the tree those Albion bastards were chopping down at the embassy. He said he'd been one once. Those SOBs turned him back into one to kill him. But why would they murder the royal wizard?"

I was trying to sort through all the threads from yesterday, but it was like someone had dumped out the sewing drawer and let all the spools roll out and tangle up all over the room.

Yet another visitor to my office from the previous day had turned up dead. If passing through my office door had somehow become the kiss of death, I'd have to make a point of inviting my ex-wife over when this was through. In the meantime, I couldn't alert the cops about Merlin and not tell them about Smook the Schnook too. And if that tree *was* Merlin, he'd been killed at the embassy. That was sovereign Albion land, which meant the cops would have no legal right to investigate inside the grounds unless invited.

I tore the sketch out of the paper and put it in my pocket.

I decided to put Merlin on the back burner for the time being. He'd appeared and disappeared inside the office, which meant no one saw him coming or going. Harvey Smook would have used the front door, and there was no shortage of skunks in the building who would turn me over to Jenkins in a heartbeat if they made the connection.

I got up to collect my coat and hat. I felt the bulge in my inside trench coat pocket, and pulled out the cash-stuffed envelope. I slipped out a hundred for myself and tossed the envelope with the rest of the dough to Mannix.

"Do whatever magic you do with that that keeps us in business, kid."

"Yes, sir. Where are you going?"

I dropped my fedora on my head and grabbed the rusty doorknob.

"I'm paying my last respects to a guy I didn't respect."

Chapter 9

Harvey Smook's office was in the business district around the corner from the courthouse. He had his name painted on the door downstairs, repeated on the directory in the lobby, again on the wall of the tenth floor under a polite arrow, and on the door to his office suite. It didn't matter how many spots he paid to hang his shingle, nor did it matter how hoity-toity the building was or how fancy his top-floor private digs were. Harvey Smook was the absolute worst private detective in town, and the only people who made the mistake of hiring him were ones who'd failed to first check with the Better Business Bureau under "P.I.'s, Worthless." And after he screwed up, they invariably won their cash back in court, which was probably why Smook had chosen that location.

The rest of us private eyes called the real shit cases "Schnook jobs," and clients that smelled like they might sue were "Schnook bait." We were like carnies with the lingo, and there was a whole Smook-generated lexicon based on the fact that Harvey Smook was the crummiest detective in the Western Hemisphere. The purpose of Smook the Schnook's existence was to make the rest of us feel better about our glamorous work of peeping in windows and rooting around in garbage cans.

I wasn't sure there'd be anyone in the offices of Harvey Smook, Private Security Agency that morning. It ended up there was not only a receptionist at the front desk, but somber organ music piping in over small speakers around the reception area.

The outpouring of affection for the deceased came as a surprise. There was exactly one bucket of carnations on a stand near the reception window, which was one more than I figured Harve Smook's death would generate. Bully for the Schnook for scrounging up someone on the planet who was sorry to see him go.

I shouldn't have laughed at his flowers. That carnation bouquet exceeded what I'd probably merit when I finally cashed in my chips. Frankly, I'd be shocked when the day came if I got more than a couple of dandelions stuffed in a two-buck shot glass, sans card, from my loyal, unpaid office staff.

The first thing I did when I got to the window was point behind the receptionist and look all surprised. When she turned around to see what I was pointing at, I filched the little envelope from the bouquet of sympathy flowers and stuffed it in my pocket.

"Yes, sir?" the confused girl asked, turning back to me. "What's wrong?"

"Just making sure Harvey's staff was maintaining the great Smook observational standards we've all come to cherish. The name's Banyon. I just stopped by to see why your boss stopped in to trash my office on the way to his rooftop swan dive."

Her somber demeanor changed to the kind of icy cold you usually only get from a dame once you've slipped a ring on her finger.

"Oh, it's *you*," she said, fuming. "You have a lot of nerve coming here, especially today. Mr. Smook finally had a case that would help him make a name for himself in this town, and you stole it from him."

"First off, Harvey Smook had a lot of names around town: loser, failure, flop, dud. As of yesterday, 'hash.' And that's just the charitable half of the alphabet. Second, I haven't had a real case in weeks. Third, no one ever stole a case from Harvey Smook because Harvey Smook never had so much as one case to steal. Fourth, Harvey Smook was only in business because his dead mother left him her dead husband's textile business which he sold to pay for everything in here, including your phony silicone torpedoes."

I felt kind of bad maligning a poor sap like the Schnook. He wasn't a bad guy, just a pathetic one. But I could see this dame was easier to operate than a can of pull-top pudding. Get her riled enough, and she'd rally to the defense of her dear deceased boss.

Like clockwork, her face turned as red as a paddy who'd forgot to pack the Irishman-Strength Noxzema Sunscreen for his Ft. Lauderdale vacation, and she swiveled in her chair and yanked a file from the nearby cabinet. I noted that there were no other files in the drawer. Poor Schnook. Pitiful even unto pancake death.

She slapped the file down in front of me and dared me with a glare to look inside which I, being the gentleman that I am, did.

"What the hell is this?" I asked, holding up the one and only sheet of paper in the folder. At the top was *H. Smook Private Security Agency, Case #1021*. (Fat chance that had any resemblance to reality. The Schnook must've figured case files were like a box of checks and started at 1000.) The single page was covered in blacked-out rectangles.

"He blocked out practically every word," I said.

"You obviously don't understand the secrecy involved in this highly sensitive business," she replied.

"I understand that you've introduced me to a miracle I never thought possible. The Schnook was an even bigger asshole dingbat than I ever gave him credit for. Is there a clean copy around here somewhere that CIA Schnook didn't black out?"

"Mr. Smook kept everything up here," she said, pressing the eraser end of a pencil through her beehive hairdo to, I could only guess, indicate where her brain would have gone if the manufacturer hadn't neglected to include one in the kit.

"So this is the big case I stole from him," I said, handing back the useless scrap of paper. "I don't suppose he told you what it was."

"Mr. Smook was very secretive about his work. I only know that he was very excited to be working on it, until he fell down the stairs and broke his leg yesterday. Then he found out that you'd swooped right in and taken over from him."

I'm a pretty easy audience for the unbelievable. The incredible becomes mundane after you've heard enough tall tales from cheating husbands standing in their underwear in motel parking lots in the middle of the night. But I admit it, this rocked me back on my heels.

Merlin had told me that the Albions' first P.I. choice had busted his leg in a fall. I'd thought about it when Mannix told me about the Schnook's crutches and broken leg, but I'd whacked that mole as soon as it poked up its head. I assumed there was no way the Albions were nuts enough to retain Harvey Smook's services. The fact that the idiot Smook had called a simple bodyguard job a "case" had thrown me.

Maybe I was just flattering myself, but it was inconceivable that I had been anyone's runner-up choice after Smook-the-goddamned-Schnook. There was only one way to deal with a revelation that cuts that deep into your soul.

"Excuse me, kitten, I'll have a belt of anything damp the Schnook has in the liquor cabinet."

She was clearly insulted at the mere suggestion. "Mr. Smook certainly did not keep alcohol at the office," the receptionist sniffed.

Okay, *now* I hated Harvey Smook.

I started to go, but suddenly remembered something. I jammed my hand in my pocket and flashed the sketch of Merlin from the morning's *Gazette*.

"Is this the guy who hired Smook?" I asked.

She gasped when she saw Merlin. "No. Certainly not. But he was in the hallway yesterday when Mr. Smook fell down the stairs. He was trying to look inconspicuous reading a magazine, but I saw him watching Mr. Smook. Mr. Smook *never* took the stairs, but that man shot some lightning out of his fingers and Mr. Smook suddenly took the fire exit instead of the elevator, then he fell. He said afterwards that the top steps turned into a slide, but they were stairs when I got there. I yelled for that man to call 911, but he was gone. Was he a cohort of yours, helping you steal Mr. Smook's big case?"

"Frankly, lady, I don't know who he was working for anymore."

I stuffed the picture of Merlin back in my pocket. I felt her eyes shooting daggers at the back of my head as I headed for the door.

"Oh, why don't you just go up to the roof and jump, like poor Mr. Smook?" she called after me.

Another unbearable surprise in a day already loaded down to the breaking point with them. I turned back to her.

"Wait, you're saying he jumped from *this* building?" I asked. "This one around us? The building you and I are standing in right now?"

I talked as slow as I possibly could without sounding like the record was set at the wrong speed. The dame was thicker than a Wendy's walrus double-cheeseburger.

"Yes, the poor, wonderful man." And then, because no one could possibly hold out any longer than this babe already had, out came the truth. "Where the hell am I gonna find another job this goddamn easy?"

I didn't give a damn about the future job prospects of the Schnook's triple-D secretary. I had a couple of new things more important to obsess over.

First, what the hell was Merlin's game? If the ditz was right he not only wasn't the Albion who'd hired the Schnook he'd deliberately taken him out of the game.

Second, it simply was not possible that the Schnook had only fallen ten floors. The body had to have dropped from a hell of a lot higher to have wound up the chop suey I'd seen at the morgue. The report had said that he'd jumped from a building on Lexington, but I'd assumed he'd gone up to the viewing platform of Olympus Towers down the corner, the favorite spot in the city for sad sack skydivers with an equal hope-to-parachute ratio. No waiting, no railing, sixty-seven floors straight down to the pavement. It was the cliché locale for the go-splat brigade, so I'd assumed a loser like Harvey Smook wouldn't buck convention. Wrong again, Banyon. Maybe the Albions were right and I wasn't as far up the P.I. food chain from Smook the Schnook as I thought.

In the hallway, I slipped out of the little envelope the card I'd filched from Harvey Smook's memorial flowers. And just like that I had another question mark thrown up in front of me like a fat broad blocking a narrow staircase.

My Dear Common Person:

*Her Royal Highness the Queen of Albion,
Supreme Governess of the Church of Albion,
Grand Duchess of East Higgledy and West
Piggledy, Distinguished Mistress of the High
Seas of Washdumpling and Warden of
Twiddlewank Glen offers Her sincerest and most
regal condolences on this, the occasion of your
tragic, yet unexceptional loss.*

Chapter 10

As a general rule I take a two-pronged approach when confronted with any situation too complicated or too risky to life and limb. Phase One: avoidance. Phase Two: alcohol. Unfortunately, this time Phase One wouldn't work. Not if someone in the Albion embassy was winding up and turning out anonymous killers to flatten me.

It had to be Jeeves. I'd asked him too much about the Merlin tree, so he sent his goon out to squash me for sticking my nose into what turned out to be the very public murder of the wizard who'd hired me. Which, given Molokai's testimony about the hooded figure who'd made the demon hurl the buttress, meant Jeeves was probably also behind the attempt on the Queen's life. What his game was, I had no idea.

I took a hit of Phase Two from my best hip flask and hailed a cab.

So everything that had happened in the past twenty-four hours was somehow connected. But if Jeeves had a henchman who could empty a parking space barehanded, why did he need to blackmail Molokai into throwing one measly chunk of church?

The answer hit me as soon as I posed the question. The hooded bastard couldn't toss the flying buttress at the Queen because he was at the event, too. Why else wouldn't Jeeves have sent him out twice to do his dirty work? So the guy in the hood wasn't just some hired muscle. There were at least two people in the Queen of

Albion's inner circle who wanted to see the bejeweled old broad dead.

It made sense. In fact, it was pretty much the only thing that made sense since I made the mistake of taking a too-easy Monday gig for too much dough.

The hack dumped me on the sidewalk in front of Wu Fong's Takeout Palace. If he'd been a bit movie actor, the cabbie's dialogue after I stiffed him on the tip would have earned him a hard R from the MPAA. He took off in a squeal of tires as I ducked down the alley to the greasy takeout joint's kitchen door.

I found Molokai sitting on a milk crate flaying dugongs. It was General Tso's Manatee Madness Month at Wu Fong's. I'd tried it a couple of times even though I knew something didn't taste right. Nothing ever tasted right at Wu Fong's. I should've figured a cheap bastard like Wu Fong would be using manatee substitute.

"What do you want, Banyon?" the demon growled when he spotted me over the bin overflowing with tail flukes and flippers.

"Your friend been back to visit you?" I demanded.

Molokai exhaled anger as he pawed a handful of dugong intestines into a bucket labeled "chop suey."

"We gonna go through this again?" the demon snarled. "I've been here working like a slave since you saw me last night. You don't believe me, go in and ask old man Wu Fong. That Chinaman's worse than Satan with the whip." He adjusted his hair net with an annoyed talon and resumed work with greater vigor.

"You've got your ear to the ground," I said. "Is there any word on the street about something going down at the Queen's stop at city hall this afternoon?"

It was the hesitation that gave him away. Just a second too long to think as he removed a spleen and dropped it in the grimy "pork fried rice" pail.

"No, I haven't heard a thing," the demon insisted.

"Molokai, I am a fan of truth-telling. I also am a fan of the phone booth on the corner. And I'm the biggest fan of all of the INS."

"Okay, okay," the demon sighed, glancing around. "All I heard is there's something happening underground. That guy that blackmailed me was talking to some people. At least according to a mole-man stopped by for an order of batter fried donkey fetlocks last night. The way he described him with the hood and hiding in the shadows, I knew it had to be the same guy. But that's *all* I know, Banyon."

So Jeeves was planning on hitting the Queen again today. If they were successful this time, she'd be the hat trick along with Harvey Smook and Merlin.

I started to leave, but the demon called after me, "Hey, that's good information, Banyon. Gotta be worth a sawbuck at least."

I only pulled a five out of my wallet and dropped it at the demon's massive feet. "Considering you nearly killed me again, our price on information has been adjusted downward."

His entire head was one big scowl, but he didn't argue. He snatched up the bill and it disappeared into the shredded rags that passed for his work smock.

"You're all heart, Banyon," I heard him mutter as I exited the alley.

That wasn't true. At this point, what with the bloating, I was mostly liver.

Wu Fong's Takeout Palace shared the alley with O'Hale's Bar. I decided to save myself a dime for the payphone and make my call to the cops from there.

I had no choice but to bring in our bungling local constabulary. I obviously couldn't contact the Albion embassy. And it didn't matter that I'd saved her life, there was no way a schlub like me was getting within a country mile of the Queen again.

I'd decided in the cab ride over that the Queen herself could not have written the note that had been included with the Schnook's memorial flowers. I'd taken a good, long look at it and it looked like it had been written with an autopen or some computer gadget, because the handwriting was too perfect to have been written by a human hand. More of Jeeves' handiwork I assumed, but why he wanted to tie the Handbag of Monmouth Palace to the death of an insignificant local P.I. I had no idea.

The welcoming gloom of O'Hale's did a better imitation of a morgue than the cold basement room across town where Harvey Smook was resting in pieces.

Ed Jaublowski had seen me come in and had already poured some varnish in a glass and slid it in front of my usual stool before I could sit down.

"Sorry about last night, Jinx," the barkeep said. "Them Temperance League broads got eyes all over every gin joint in town these days, you know?"

"Gimme the phone and a couple free rounds and we'll call it square."

"Yeah, sure thing." Jaublowski passed the phone up from behind the bar and slid it next to my liquid lunch.

"Pretzels, too. The closest I've come to eating anything solid in the past twenty-four hours was a Pathfinder bumper."

I called Precinct #1, but the whole place had pretty much hung up an out-to-lunch sign. There was nobody to speak to from my old cop days. I even bit the bullet and tried Jenkins, but he was already mismanaging the scene at city hall. After the attempt on the Queen's life at St. Regent's they'd be on high alert, but they had no idea that a hit was definitely coming and that it'd be from below this time. I'd have to get down there.

I made another quick call, this one to the florist whose name had been embossed on the planter in Smook's office. I hoped Jeeves or his partner had paid personally for the flowers because it'd give me a direct link from the Albion scumbag to Smook, which linked to everything else that had been going on the past day. It'd be a hell of a lot easier to lay it out for Jenkins when I tried to get him to slap the cuffs on the rat bastard. But after some fast-talking on my part I only turned up that the note had been delivered by a young courier from the embassy. The florist hadn't billed a credit card, but had been paid in weasel skins and silk, which was the official Albion currency until 1872 and was still sometimes used by officials directly representing the Queen and royal family.

It would've been nice to catch Jeeves in the act but he was slipperier than a bowl of guts and mucus pudding, the traditional Albion Christmas dessert. I slugged down what was left in my glass, emptied the bowl of stale pretzels into my pocket for the trip across town, and hightailed it for the nearest subway station.

The line usually ran straight to city hall, but because of the Queen's visit I was booted out at Burr Street Station near the interdimensional portal to the mirror-universe Earth where the hippie revolution was actually successful until they accidentally wiped out the entire human race when President Hendrix dropped a love bomb on Vietnam in 1971 and infected the whole planet with syphilis.

I had to hoof double-time all the way to city hall's shiny silver dome with the phoenix on top. The roof stuck out from the other drab government buildings dead center of midtown by dint of its unrelenting ugliness.

The streets were packed with spectators desperate to catch a glimpse of some old bat they didn't know from a hole in the wall. These same applauding asshole gawkers probably never visited elderly old ladies they were actually related to but who they'd stashed away for safe keeping in some lousy nursing home. People are bastards.

Speaking of old ladies, I found Jenkins hollering instructions, no doubt staggeringly dimwitted ones, into a radio over on the sidewalk on the building's south side. He looked exhausted, but his baggy-eyed face lit up when he spotted me.

"Banyon. I've been thinking about you," the flatfoot announced. His handcuffs were already in his hand. "I got an interesting call from Harvey Smook's secretary. Looks like I'm going to be having a little chat with you about your dead P.I. pal after all."

"Let's save us both the hassle on the false arrest lawsuit front, Jenkins. Your own report gives time of death as 5:30 last night. Same report says dozens of witnesses saw Smook the Schnook slap asphalt at exactly that time. At 5:30 last night, I was with you on top of St. Regent's. You probably didn't notice the time because observation never has been your strong suit, detective, but your forensics team would have."

Judging by the cop's suddenly dyspeptic expression, he realized that he was my alibi for the Schnook's death. The cuffs went away and his lip curled.

"Yeah, okay. Then get the hell out of here. But don't go far. I still want to talk to you about Smook after we get this circus squared away."

A ripple of excitement suddenly started east of midtown down Fahrenheit Boulevard in the direction of the Albion Embassy. A cheer rose from the crowd. Little Albion flags waved all along the parade route, as if the crowd was welcoming an army of liberating American doughboys instead of some old foreign bag in a glass slipper led by a bunch of official carriages, pumpkins and limos.

Just my luck. The royal biddy had shown up early.

"You've got to radio that slipper to turn around, Jenkins," I said.

The crowd was contained by yellow sawhorse barriers along the jam-packed sidewalks, and a million hands flung the traditional rose pedals and swan beaks out into the road beneath the Queen's passing glass shoe.

"What?" Jenkins said. "The hell I will."

"There's going to be another attempt today, from underground this time," I snapped. "I got a demon source heard it straight from a mole-man. Turn that slipper around right now, Jenkins, or this crowd of beak-tossing lemmings will be combing diamonds and dead Queen slurry out of their hair for a month."

I don't give Dan Jenkins much credit because he doesn't deserve much. But my urgency was infectious, turning this into one of those exceptional times where a pinprick opened up the narrowest escape route to the dormant lobe in his brain where he'd locked away what little common sense he possessed. The flatfoot kept a beady eye on me as he slowly slipped his radio from the pocket of his raincoat.

"Jenkins here--"

That was all he managed to get out.

Jenkins was barely capable of dealing with the world he could see. As it was, he'd been concerned about security on the street and the surrounding buildings. "Down" was hardly a blip on his radar. Since the previous day's attack on the Queen had come from above, he had positioned every SWAT team and plainclothes cop on rooftops and in windows all around the parade route. Even the uniforms at ground level were watching the sky. No one was prepared when the road suddenly buckled up as if hit by a massive punched fist underneath the pair of motorcycle cops directly in front of the royal slipper.

If the explosion was aiming for the Queen the bombers missed by two car lengths. The coachman at the front of the slipper yanked on the reins and the team of white horses clomped to a stop. The driver pulled a handle at his side and the slipper behind him slammed on the brakes. I could see Her Royal Evening Bag frozen in mid-wave as she watched with dull incomprehension the scene playing out before her.

The street rose on the ripple of the unseen hand shoving up hard from below, and the two lead motorcycles rose up and rode the cracking asphalt like surfers riding a wave. The front tire of one caught a blossoming crevice in the road that sent him tumbling off his bike, the other skidded straight through the crowd and into the display window of Beacon's Department Store.

The street rose high and settled back down fast. A thick cloud of dust belched high into the air as the shattered pavement settled into a fresh hole.

The crowd took it all in with a sort of stunned stoicism. Hey, when you live in the city, you see a lot worse than a sudden sinkhole on the way to pick up a pack of stogies at the corner market. The first thing on everybody's mind was probably that it was a gas main explosion. The second was how, given local government's usual rapid response to a major traffic hazard, the mess in the street was going to screw up their respective commutes for the next five to seven years. The calm lasted right up until a huge figure came scurrying up from the depths of the newly formed hole and into the fresh air.

The gathered multitude went from zero to berserk in three seconds.

Everybody knew that alligators had been living in the sewers for decades. Over time, they'd gone albino and nearly blind from lack of sun, which was probably lousy from their perspective. On the other hand, they'd become super-intelligent thanks to all the genetically modified and irradiated gunk we'd been flushing down and marinating them in. They'd lately set up a rudimentary feudal system which, according to a recent series of articles by the *Gazette*'s sewer beat reporter, was being challenged by a powerful gator who had declared himself King Chompy I.

The alligator that slipped out of the hole in the road and scurried across the street had King Chompy's banner tied to the end of his tail and he dragged it behind him.

The crowd screamed and ran, shoving everything and everyone -- cops, barricades, one another, Soylent Green vendors -- out of the way in a mad dash from the scampering gator. The team of horses reared wildly, and the coachman slapped the flat of his palm down on an emergency release that cut the harnesses. The freed horses stampeded away with the panicking crowd. The coachman scurried down from his perch and ran like mad back in the direction from which the slipper had come.

"Take him out! Take the alligator out!" Jenkins screamed into his walkie-talkie.

But if the half-blind alligator had meant to go for the Queen, he missed his target by a country mile. As sniper bullets pinged off his genetically-enhanced hide, he scurried straight past the royal slipper to a yellow fire hydrant on the sidewalk. He promptly bit the side off the hydrant and, as water gushed in an arc across the road, scurried straight past the royal slipper a second time and back to the open hole.

"*Vivat Rex Chompy!*" the alligator howled, although since they'd only recently developed vocal chords his raspy voice didn't carry far over the screaming crowd.

Sniper bullets continued to pelt his sides, and he left a slick trail of blood as he slipped back into the hole with one mighty sweep of his thrashing tale.

Men were scrambling out of pumpkins that had stopped dead in the street. Some were Albion security, and the weapons of these were drawn as they ran.

The Queen sat seemingly unharmed in her carriage.

The water arced over the street and splashed the roof of the giant glass slipper in which the ample butt of Albion's two hundred-plus year old Queen sat on gilded cushions.

The carriage was bulletproof, but obviously not waterproof. There was water pooling around the Queen's feet and I saw a thin waterfall running down the inside walls from the roof. The dame was lucky again. She'd get a little damp, but not a lot dead.

Everyone else was watching the Queen, but nearby a fat man in striped trousers caught my eye. I had seen him on the dais at the cathedral the day before, but I had no idea who he was. Just some high-level nobleman pasty-face with a musty title, no chin, and a pair of siblings for parents. Both of the Albionman's hands were pressed to his lower lip, fingers curled tight, as he watched the Queen's slipper fill with water. His face was ashen, his eyes wide and he was shaking with terror.

"She can't get wet! For the love of God, she must stay completely dry!"

When he started yelling, I figured at first he was the royal hairdresser or maybe the Queen's personal seamstress. Either way, he could've cooled his jets. The water level was rising so slowly that the men who were racing up to the slipper would get there long before the blue rinse in the royal coif was in danger of running. As for the dress, if the white lace on the powder blue number she was wearing was trashed by the rising tide around her ankles, she could always sell off a castle or two to buy a replacement.

I was distracted from the screaming Albionman by a sudden flash down the street.

It came from the direction of the Queen's carriage. It was blinding even in daylight, like the flash that comes from a transformer blowing up. But there was no accompanying explosion. The only sound was a sort of muffled *tharrump*.

I looked over in time to see the interior of the Queen's bulletproof slipper flooding with dark gray smoke. The Queen's expression was glazed, and her head pivoted from left to right multiple times rapidly before her face vanished behind the deep fog.

Jenkins had his walkie-talkie back up and was barking orders. "There's been some kind of malfunction with the slipper. Get an ambulance up here, fast. Alert Sloan-Frankenstein Hospital that the Queen's coming in; tell them that they might have to treat for possible smoke inhalation."

A second *tharrump*, this one louder than the first. The ground rumbled and back at the glass slipper puffs of smoke escaped like steam from the seams of a boiler that was ready to blow. The fat Albionman was kneeling in the street now, weeping openly and pulling at his threads of white hair as he stared in abject horror at the Queen's carriage.

You work in this business long enough you get an instinct when something's wrong. I'm not patting myself on the back. There were probably three dozen old-timer cops around the city hall plaza that got the same feeling I got at that moment. Unlucky for them, their boss was the moron with the walkie-talkie standing next to me.

"Get everyone away from that slipper, Jenkins," I warned.

The cop just shot me a glare and continued barking orders.

Another *tharrump* from the carriage and more pressurized smoke fired angrily from the seams. The giant glass bow on the toe fell off and shattered in the street.

The Queen was still invisible inside, but the armed Albions who had been racing to the slipper abruptly lost their nerve. They'd all either slowed or stopped outright, and one of the security guys had his finger pressed to a receiver in his ear and was conferring with someone higher up the food chain.

"Call your snipers, Jenkins," I said. "Tell them to take down whatever it is comes out of that carriage."

"Look, Banyon--" the flatfoot began, but he was cut off by the final tharrump.

The door exploded off the carriage, trailing smoke as it soared across the street and shattered against the side of the Grimm Bros. Insurance Company Building.

A latticework of fissures erupted all around the glass slipper carriage. It sounded like rapidly cracking ice that had been dropped in a too-warm glass of bourbon (assuming you're a teenaged girl who thinks bourbon is grape goddamn Kool-Aid.)

The Queen's slipper exploded in a million tinkling shards of glass that scattered across pavement, sidewalks and the suits of the nearby security men who were suddenly crouching, hands over their heads as they watched the cloud of smoke dissipate.

The Queen stood alone inside the skeletal remains of the slipper, water from the spraying hydrant soaking her dress and pouring to the ground from around her feet.

Her head continued to swivel unnaturally east to west. It suddenly spun a couple of very fast complete 360 rotations, which was a physical impossibility that even the most aggressive European royal inbreeding probably couldn't have managed. The head whirled around a few more times before it locked back in the traditional front-facing direction. The royal mouth was open but when she spoke her lips didn't move. Her voice was amplified and sounded like thunder blasting out of a staticky megaphone.

"*We are not amused!*" the Queen of Albion announced.

She held her hands out, arms bent at the elbows. Her balled fists retracted up her arms and twin barrels appeared from her wrists. Her head began to pivot left then right as twin jets of flame erupted from her royal wrist stumps.

The blast of fire caught the nearest security man, who erupted in a ball of screaming flames -- although with that swishy Albion accent it was more like flaming screams -- as he ran to the gushing hydrant to douse his double-breasted Saville Row bonfire.

"*We are Albion! We like chips!*" the Queen bellowed.

Her Majesty's flamethrowers blasted across the road and took out the front of Grimm Bros. Insurance. Picture windows instantly melted to slag in the intense heat.

The Queen was a pretty spry old gal for 236 as she hopped down to the street. Somewhere during the jump her flamethrowers retracted and her hands returned. She wrapped her fingers around the chassis of her carriage and raised it over her head, flinging it at her retreating armed guards. Two of the men were flattened by the rolling slipper and dragged into the sinkhole made by the subterranean albino alligators.

When she picked up the mayor's limo and flung it through a second story apartment with the Albion flag hanging out the window, I knew for sure that my attacker the previous night had been the Robot Queen of Albion in an Old Navy hooded sweatshirt.

She was the right height and shape. She'd been on the dais at St. Regent's Drive-Thru Cathedral and so couldn't have thrown that chunk of church at herself. The deal sealer was the way she picked up two sedans, one right after another, and heaved them at a SWAT team van that had just rounded the corner. The first hurled car ripped the back off the SWAT van and the second crushed the cab.

Jenkins and I took cover along with a dozen other spectators behind the marble fountain statue of Sally Jesse Raphael at the edge of city hall plaza.

"Subdue, subdue!" Jenkins was yelling into his radio. "Do not shoot the Queen! Repeat, do not shoot the Queen!"

"That's not the Queen!" I snapped. "It's obviously a robot. By my count, it's killed at least seven people so far and who knows how many more in those buildings and SWAT van."

A city bus suddenly bounced past us in a terrible crunch of metal and shattering glass, like a kid's tossed Tonka truck. Luckily, no one in town used hippie public transportation so the only body bouncing around inside was the dead bus driver.

"Eight," I amended. "Shoot the bastard thing while you can."

In the middle of the ruined street, water arcing dramatically behind her, the Robot Queen's head rose six inches on a retractable turret and spun one very slow 360 degree rotation. Her Robotic Majesty raised her arms, emitted a low static roar, then shouted past unmoving lips: "*We are Albion! Communications port invalid or busy! Control, alt, delete! Save file! Kill, kill, kill!*"

Beats me if Jenkins, the consummate civil servant, would have made the right decision before the old robot dame could level all of midtown. Fortunately somebody else up the cop food chain took the decision out of his sweaty hands. The order to fire came down through every radio in the square from the chief himself, and it was suddenly the Fourth of July with screaming lead raining down from every direction.

The Queen let loose a screech that shrieked feedback through every speaker around city hall plaza. Cell phones in pockets vibrated and spontaneously burst into flames. Cops and civilians flapped at their burning clothes even as the old robot gal stopped hollering and plastered her arms to the sides of her powder blue Bob Mackie original.

Her spine split open along the back seam of her dress and a retractable jet pack slid into view. As bullets continued to rain down all around her, digging asphalt dimples in the road, the pack on her back ignited and the Robot Queen launched skyward on a plume of smoke and flame. The air conditioner hum from the rocket on her back faded in the distance as she tore off in a fiery arc over the Randolph Office Building and disappeared into the metal canyons of the city.

The gunfire stopped and the plaza grew as quiet as a ghost tiptoeing on feather pillows through Marshmallow Cemetery near Lollipop Grove over by the interstate.

Jenkins looked rattled. I didn't blame him. I had some serious questions of my own. As long as he was there, I asked my cop pal the first and most important one on my mind.

"You still do those hotline rewards for caring citizens who bring tips to the cops?" I asked as I got to my feet and used my fedora to smack away the dust on the knees of my slacks. "If so, give me most of mine in fifties, but throw in one sawbuck for cab fare, Detective Jenkins."

Chapter 11

Turns out there's no more rewards from the cops for stoolies and busybodies. Most police departments cancelled their cash incentives to squealers after some witch in Westport, Connecticut got ticked at the lady across the street for always peeping in her windows. She boiled the old busybody in a stew and fed her to her husband's ad exec boss and a prospective client. Her husband landed the big business account and the witch got the chair. The Kravitz Rule was enacted all over the country after I quit the cops. I don't know how I missed hearing about that one. I get all the shit luck.

By the next morning, all hell had broken loose. The survivors and family members of the deceased victims of the Robot Queen attack were screaming bloody murder. The twenty-four hour cable channels were doing their best to churn up the blood in the water. Since Albion was a crucial ally against the United Arab-Martian-Commie League, Washington was trying to walk the tightrope between demanding answers while downplaying the incident. Over in Monmouth Palace in the capital of Vauxhall, the Albion royal family had so far issued only one short, official statement:

We regret the actions of our robot and we are looking into the incident.

You had to be impressed by the bloodlessness of those Albion sons of bitches. The average family over there must save a bundle on their annual refrigeration bill. One ice-cold "I love you" from mumsy to daddy and last night's leftover sheep's stomach stuffed with cow intestines stays frozen for a year.

At least it wasn't all frost and gastroenteritis over there. A fortune was paid yearly by Albion taxpayers to keep the royal family in satin pantaloons, and thousands had taken to the streets of Vauxhall demanding to know the whereabouts of the real Queen. Hundreds of cell phone store and supermarket owners were terrified that it was the Robo-Queen that had cut the ribbons at their grand openings, which would render their stores officially unrecognized by the crown and their owners subject to the death penalty, usually by mallet and administered by Albion's last surviving giant.

The Queen, if she was at the palace at all, remained far from the street-side windows. According to the story I'd seen on the TV that morning, all the mob had gotten so far was Prince Gormless, the Queen's oldest son and heir to the throne, sticking his massive nose and giant, crooked choppers through the gates of Monmouth Palace to assure the citizenry that the monarchy was as strong as ever. He was sent flouncing back to the palace covered in rotten tomatoes and batter fried fish.

On my way to the office, I'd filched a newspaper someone had carelessly neglected to collect from their stoop. I slapped the copy of the *Gazette* onto my desk as I dropped into my chair. I did my best to ignore the noises from the agitated mice banging around inside the walls with icepacks on their heads.

SHE'S A KILLER QUEEN! blared the headline.

I hadn't seen any press on the scene of the massacre, but there had sure been plenty of photographers because there were all kinds of photos of Her Robotic Majesty crushing the American peasantry with carelessly tossed cars and blasting off into the stratosphere in her rocket-powered blue Bob Mackie and matching Rumpelstiltskin shoes.

According to the paper, the Robot Queen had touched down a couple of times during the night to raze some fish and chip joints, but where she'd gone to afterwards was anyone's guess. All eyes were on the Albion Embassy now, but she hadn't returned there.

There wasn't much in the paper that I didn't already know. I'd flipped over to the sports section to check out the bear-baiting scores when I heard my outer door open.

I knew it was too much to imagine that my secretary had decided to come into work that morning, so I wasn't surprised when Mannix poked his head into my office.

"Good morning, Mr. Crag," the elf said. "Can I get you some coffee and Good 'n' Plenty?"

"You can get me Johansen," I said. "It's tomorrow again. When are the exterminators coming?" The elf's expression grew even cheerier than usual. "Mr. Bob told me this morning that they will maybe be here this afternoon," Mannix replied.

"That's a new one. Johansen's doctor must have told him his enlarged heart is ready to go supernova. No surprise there. A billion well-placed chilidogs will do it. But if he thinks he's getting out of hiring an exterminator because he's planning on being dead before lunch, the cardiac arrest won't be his last shock. I've got a valkyrie owes me a favor. I can have his fat soul hauled back out of Asgard as soon as I can find a forklift that won't snap under the weight."

Mannix didn't know what to say, so all he did was smile and shrug. The kid liked Johansen. Mannix liked *everybody*, didn't matter if they were skunks or rats or lying Norse whale landlords. One day I was going to have to address that deficiency in the poor kid's personality.

Not that day, though. I still had some mental knots to untie, and there was only one sure way to loosen up the most stubborn tangles.

"I'll take that coffee," I said. "No cream, no sugar, no coffee." I slapped a Jackson on my desk. "Cheapest bottle of coffee at Arnie's."

Mannix didn't take the bill. Instead, he slipped without a word into Doris' office and returned a moment later with a brown paper bag and a disapproving frown.

"It's naughty to drink alcohol this early in the day," the elf chided as he slid the twenty off the desk and the bag onto it.

"Tell that to the New Amsterdam Spirits Company softball team and the uniforms paid for by my generous contributions."

I uncapped the bottle and grabbed my mug from the windowsill.

"You'll be pleased to know, Mannix, that your charming employer isn't as worthless as circumstances briefly appeared to indicate," I said as I poured.

The truth had come out once the insanity had died down outside city hall and Jenkins had me hauled back to the stationhouse.

Before the Queen's visit, the Albion advance team had asked for a list of every P.I. in town, ranked best to worst. What Jeeves told me was true, at least as far as it went. They had wanted a P.I. near the stage. Jeeves had fed the cops the same line, and a bunch of the brass had submitted lists. But when the Albions had selected their man, a lot of the cops were shocked they'd picked Harvey Smook for the job.

"Jeeves wanted a screw-up near the stage," I explained to Mannix. "He wanted the phony Queen exposed for some reason. I guess Merlin found out and took Smook out. Didn't kill him, just put him on the injured list. So Jeeves needed a pinch-hitter at the last minute. Jenkins was working close with Jeeves by that point setting up the security at St. Regent's. Jenkins admitted that Jeeves asked him at the last minute who the worst P.I. in town was, and sweetheart Jenkins of course nominated me. Jenkins let it spill that Jeeves told him he didn't want someone who'd outshine the locals. So Jeeves thought he was getting a dud who'd just stand there like the Schnook would have as the Robot Queen got flattened. Instead, he got me. Excelsior."

I took a belt from my mug. I admit it. I make one hell of a cup of coffee.

"Do you want me to type all this up and close the file?" Mannix asked.

"Sure," I said. "Leave out that jackass 'excelsior' bullshit. But we're closing the file. I'm out of it now. The Robo-Queen with her rocket pack obviously hauled Harvey Smook about a mile above his building after he left here and let him drop. That's how he was so splattered-up from what appeared at first to only be a ten-story fall. Doc Minto autopsied the remains and he backed me up on the height. I sicced Detective Moron Jenkins on Jeeves as the prime suspect. Whatever else the Albions are up to, it's got nothing to do with Banyon Investigations. File away."

I raised my mug magnanimously and waved the elf away. Mannix ducked out the door and a moment later I heard the rapid clatter and dings of Doris' Smith-Corona.

It's not often I get through a caper with as few scrapes and bruises as this one. The cops were on the big case. The embassy was stonewalling. Not my business.

I did feel bad for Merlin. The dead wizard obviously wanted me up near the stage. He'd made all the arrangements, and Jeeves had cashed in the old conjurer's chips as a reward for his meddling. Maybe he didn't know it was Jeeves, but the wizard must've figured out somebody was determined to unmask the Robot Queen as a phony and wanted to ensure the great Albion secret was kept. What happened to the real Queen, if she was living or dead, wasn't my concern.

At least I'd been right about the note on the flowers at Harvey Smook's office. I knew it had been too perfect, like it had been written by some computerized gizmo. The robot must have been programmed to copy the Queen's handwriting. Chalk another win up for the guy who was no longer the worst living detective in town.

For the first time I noticed that my office had been restored to its normal cluttered state. The files were off the floor and everything that the rampaging Smook the Schnook had swept off my desk had been replaced.

Despite my cockiness, there were still a few nagging loose ends flapping around at the back of my brain that I was hoping to snip off with a pair of booze scissors. It's the small things that drive me the most nuts. Mice in the walls. Pixies and imps. Don't even get me started on midgets. What had been bothering me since I left Precinct #1 last night was why Jeeves had ordered Harvey Smook killed.

Sending the Robot Queen out to crush me under a Mercedes was easy to understand. I'd witnessed them cutting down the Merlin tree and might have put two-and-two together. But Merlin had benched Smook before St. Regent's. The Schnook couldn't have known anything that was damaging to Jeeves. So why turn him to hash?

I poured myself another cup of lethal coffee and savored the rich Columbian flavor via the oak barrels of the Jack Daniel's distillery.

As I put down the bottle, I noticed sitting next to my phone the book Merlin had dropped off two days before. A piece of paper hung out between the pages. It must've gotten knocked loose when Harvey Smook pitched his fit in the office.

I slipped the paper out and glanced a contented eye over it. By the time I was done reading, I was a hell of a lot less content and grabbing for my bottle of Folger's.

"Mannix, how much of that cash I gave you did you deposit?" I hollered.

The typewriter stopping dinging and Mannix hopped back into my office carrying the bankbook from Doris' desk. "All nineteen hundred and fifty dollars," the elf said, holding the book up for me to inspect.

I remembered I'd pulled out a hundred before I gave the elf the rest of the four grand. I fished in my wallet and found the bill. The hundred was now a fifty. A total of two thousand dollars had vanished in a puff of smoke.

"Dammit." I held up the scrap of paper. "Did Smook see this? It was in the book."

"Yes, Mr. Crag. When he knocked the things off your desk, he saw that fall out of the book. He said something about the Queen on the cover and picked that paper up to read it. He was very, very angry when he first came here, but he was less angry when he left, once he read that. He seemed very excited when he ran out the door, like a good little boy who's just found the bicycle he wanted underneath the Christmas tree."

I slumped back in my chair, crumpling the note in my hand. "I should know by now, Mannix, that the minute I think I've come out ahead is the exact moment I need to break out my galoshes and umbrella for the inevitable typhoon-level Banyon shit-storm."

I shook out the letter and started reading.

My Dear Mister Banyon,

I am pleased that you have accepted our offer to safeguard the "Queen" while she is visiting your fine city. Welcome to the team! First, up, by accepting the Cursed Ruby of Pimlico or its monetary equivalent, you have agreed to the terms herein.

The curse of the Pimlico Ruby is a fascinating one, dating back to St. Arterius the Pauper, also known as St. Aterius the Hideously Mutilated and, at the very end, St. Arterius the Horrifyingly Dead. If you fail to keep up your end of the bargain, the curse will rid you of half its own value every twenty-four hours until it eventually halves our initial agreed payment to nothing. Once that has occurred, if you still have not succeeded in your mission, the curse will go after your personal wealth and future earnings. Eventually, this will render you destitute. Without cash or property to liquidate, it will attack all you have left: you. This will be accomplished by falling safe, trolley car accident, surgical error or any of a thousand other possibilities -- the precise details are for the curse to decide. Sadly, most recipients of the Cursed Ruby of Pimlico don't survive the initial halving process. None have survived the second. I do hope, Mr. Banyon, that this will give you incentive to do the job for which you've been hired to the jolly well best of your ability. We're talking you giving 110% here. (Which, after twenty-four hours will be whittled down to 55%, and 27.5% the next day. You get the idea).

I stopped reading and checked my watch. It was about two days to the minute since Merlin had gotten up to leave the office. I checked my wallet again. The fifty that was there a few minutes before was now twenty-five measly bucks.

"I can guess what Smook did after he read the rest of this," I said, scanning the bottom of the letter. "Merlin says here that he thinks Jeeves is working for somebody who has it in for the Queen and that he can't go to the cops because of the scandal. There's some garbage about putting in a good word about a knighthood if I expose the plot. Smook must've run right to a payphone to call the embassy after he read this, and Jeeves sent the robot out to pancake him."

"Now that you mention it, I did see the angry man on the payphone down the street right after he left here. That's when I went out to pick up your...special refreshment." Mannix nodded to the bottle on my desk.

"Thanks for reminding me, kid." I skipped the glass and this time took a swig straight out of the refreshment bottle.

When I put the bottle down I heard frantic scampering near my foot and glanced down to find a couple of furry rodents in turtlenecks trying to climb a stalk of celery they'd propped up against the leg of my desk. Their little paws were shaking with the DTs and their bloodshot black eyes were fixated on the Holy Grail neck of the booze bottle, which was all they could see jutting up from their angle on the floor.

I gave the little rats a kick that sent them sliding halfway to my couch. They booked it straight for the hole in the wall in the back of the closet, muttering mousy imprecations the whole way home. My impending vivisection wasn't enough. Despite everything else, I still wanted to know why those damn little bastards had suddenly taken up residence in the walls of my rundown office.

I grabbed up Merlin's letter once more.

"You know, Mannix, you have to be impressed by the universal awfulness of Smook the Schnook's rotten luck. If he'd called the embassy ten minutes earlier, Jeeves and the fake Queen would've probably still been at St. Regent's, Jeeves would've missed the call, and Harvey Smook might not right now be a bowl of Jell-O jiggling in the morgue." I placed the letter in the center of my desk and slid it very slowly off the far side until it fluttered to the floor. "Smook must've ratted out Merlin to Jeeves too, so Jeeves treed the wizard and had him chopped into cordwood. Probably professional jealousy kept Smook from telling Jeeves about me and this note, but I walked into that buzz saw all by myself when I stopped by the embassy to play good Samaritan. And look at that--" I waved vaguely to where the note had fallen. "Every time he mentions the Queen he puts her in quotes. He means the Robot Queen. There's no wiggle room for me. Your boss and pal, Mannix, is well and rightly screwed."

Mannix had picked up the letter from the floor. He furrowed his little brow as he read it carefully, and I could see he was putting that elf brain of his on DEFCON One as he considered my little -- and growing littler, according to my wallet -- problem.

"Well," the elf finally decided, placing the note carefully back to my desk, "under these special, very bad circumstances, even though it's not twelve o'clock yet, maybe it isn't so naughty for you to drink as much alcohol as possible after all."

You had to love the crackerjack office staff at Banyon Investigations.

I crumpled the letter and tossed it into the wastebasket. It, of course, bounced off all the crap that was already crammed in there and landed on the floor.

I took another belt of coffee and thought of life with half my body in a garbage can out behind Vincetti's fish market and the rest of me propped up on phonebooks in my chair waiting another day for the final ax to fall. According to the terms of the contract I'd unwittingly agreed to, it could be a literal ax that hacked me in half. Wizard bastard.

I had planned on taking the afternoon off and wasting it betting on the cockroach races at O'Hale's. Now it wasn't even noon and already I had to save the whole Albion monarchy as well as my own sorry hide.

"What day is it today?" I asked.

"Wednesday," Mannix replied.

I finished my coffee and dragged my tired carcass out of my chair. "New hours at Banyon Investigations starting next week. If I get through this in one piece, from now on we're closed on goddamned Wednesdays too."

Chapter 12

I figured Jeeves was my best bet to start. The Albion High Whizboom for Her Majesty's External Matters had made it his secret mission to expose the Robot Queen to the world, and so he was at the center of this whole mess. I didn't know if he was the scumbag behind the plot or if, as Merlin suspected, he had a boss. The guy had stooge written all over his pasty face, but so did every Albionman. Still, if I could pin back his wings, I could get him to spill the beans on anyone else who might be involved.

I took along Merlin's book. The wizard had told me it was background reading, and even though I generally preferred to wing it, I also preferred my legs and lower torso in their current attached state. Call me a softy, but I'm real sentimental about all my limbs that way: legs, arms...I don't play favorites.

The letter that explained the contract I'd agreed to when I accepted that damned Pimlico Ruby as payment had been hidden in the book, and since the letter was important Merlin must've thought the book he'd stashed it in for safekeeping was pretty important too.

I cracked open the old leather volume on the subway ride across town.

# # #

Once Upon A Time *in an age long ago there lived an agreeable young princess who, after being an agreeable young princess for a happy little while, became a pleasant young Queen.*

The empire of the Pleasant Queen covered a vast area of the whole of all the wide world: oceans and continents and islands and sky. Her father, the Dead King, had lived one hundred and seventy-two years, and although long lives were quite an ordinary thing in her family, she understood that death would one day claim her, either in old age or perhaps even before that. Any night at the symphony a whalebone could accidentally spring from her corset and pierce her heart or any day on the street someone could accidentally drop a horse on her. The Pleasant Queen wisely knew that one day, by God's hand or by Man's, she would die.

"I must have an heir," she announced one day at court. "As my father, the Dead King, had me, so too must I have one pleasant like me, the Pleasant Queen, who is suitable to take over my kingdom when I am gone."

So the royal surgeons were summoned, the most wise and learned men in all the great kingdom. And these wise and learned men did snip a little bit off that part of the Pleasant Queen's most royal queenly person that made babies. This essence from the Queen was that which made a princess a queen or a prince a king. This shimmering bit from the Pleasant Queen was hurried to the royal gardens and buried deep in a bed of rich loam in the brightest, warmest corner of the sausage patch. The next morning, the royal surgeons were delighted to find a squalling infant boy rolling in the dirt, and they hurried to deliver the firstborn child and prince of the realm to the Pleasant Queen.

"Oh, my, what are those things on its head?" the Pleasant Queen asked. "Is it ill? Can it fly? They are most frightening and unappealing and most assuredly not regal."

"Those are the prince's royal ears, your majesty," they replied.

"Oh, my, and what are those things in its mouth? Oh, dear, he has been given novelty teeth by the royal jester. He will choke most frightfully dead on them. Have the jester Yorick pressed between two very large, flat rocks as a lesson to the rest of the tumblers and fools of the Jester's Guild, Local 170, to keep their props from the mouths of royal babes," the Pleasant Queen instructed.

"Majesty, those are the prince's own royal, regal teeth.'

"Oh," the Pleasant Queen said. "Oh, my, oh, dear.

Get it a nanny and put it somewhere in the back of the palace before someone sees it. Perhaps it will grow into its ghastly giant ears and comic-tragic teeth."

The tiny prince grew into a slightly larger prince but, lamentably his ears and teeth continued to grow right along with the rest of him. Even more lamentably, the prince's brain did not. And so the firstborn son of the Pleasant Queen was called Prince Gormless.

"Oh, dear, oh, my," the Pleasant Queen said. "My firstborn son and heir to my kingdom is an idiot child. I cannot subject my subjects to a king so dim of bulb and large of ear, who looks like he is chewing on a piano from the royal conservatory and could hang glide to France. I shall have to try again, harder this time, to make a prince who will become a king worthy of my people."

And so it was that the royal surgeons were summoned a second time. Again, a shimmering bit was snipped from the Queen's person and buried in a different part of the sausage patch, and the next day a new baby was brought before the Queen.

"Oh, dear, oh, my," the Pleasant Queen said. "Only on a horse or mule from the royal stables or on this one's brother, Prince Gormless, who is over there in the corner having an argument with the cat, have I seen such ivory obscenities. Take it and put it in the care of another nanny somewhere even further in the back of the palace."

The small baby grew into the second prince of the Pleasant Queen's kingdom. Whenever he was around little things would disappear from around the palace and turn up in the strangest of places, like the pockets of thieves and the local pawn shop over on the corner of Peasant Lane and Sheep Street. What was more, the Queen did note that the little friends her second child brought home to court play dates were of surprisingly low moral character for babies. And so it was that the second prince was called Prince Thieving.

"Oh, dear, oh, my," the Pleasant Queen lamented. "Two sons have I now, and neither are fit to lead my kingdom after I am gone. I shall have to try again for a worthy king to sit upon the throne of my father, the Dead King."

And so a third time the royal surgeons were summoned, and a third time a bit to make a baby was snipped from the Pleasant Queen and carried in haste to the royal gardens. This time the surgeons had selected the most shimmering and the most queenly bit of all, and it was planted over with the flowers instead of in the sausage patch in hope of avoiding the terrible, giant, crooked teeth of Prince Gormless and Prince Thieving, as well as their less tangible but no less troubling traits of personality.

The next day the surgeons brought a new, third baby prince before the Pleasant Queen. This latest infant child did not have the ears or teeth of his older brothers, which was a good sign to the Pleasant Queen, but sad experience had made Her Majesty cautious.

"Nanny. Back of the palace. And keep an eye on it."

This third prince grew into a young man who liked the company of other young men a little too much, if thou knowest what I mean.

"Oh, dear, oh, my," the Pleasant Queen said. "How were the royal surgeons to know that by selecting such a queenly bit and planting it in the pansy patch they would make him light in the crackows? I shall tell you how they should know. They are royal surgeons and are paid the pelts of only the most noble of weasels and the finest silks to know such things, that's how. Off with the quacksalvers' heads!"

And so the heads of the royal surgeons were indelicately amputated by sword and placed on spikes outside the kingdom walls to frighten the Twinkie-poos away.

"Oh, dear, oh, my," the Pleasant Queen said at last. "My surgeons are all dead and all of my shimmering bits to make babies have been used up. My three sons are unworthy of the throne of my father, the Dead King. What am I, his daughter, the Pleasant Queen, to do?"

And so the Pleasant Queen summoned her three sons, who were now grown into men, more or less, before her throne and informed them of her intentions.

"Though age and infirmity weaken us," the Pleasant Queen informed the princes gathered in her throne room. "Though our eyes grow dim and our hearing poor, and though our joints swell and our spine bend. Though we develop a very large, unsightly hump on our back, and though we sometimes might take hours to remember where we lay down the keys to the royal coach. Even if we must force our frail body to shuffle on for a thousand years in the gray twilight between living and death, we will see one of you succeed us to the throne of our father, the Dead King, over our dead, regal body."

And so it is to this very day that the three Princes, judged unworthy by their mother, can only gaze upon the throne that would never be theirs unless the Pleasant Queen was accidentally impaled by a flying wicket at a cricket match or flattened outside the palace gates by a runaway roasted chestnut cart.

#

By the time my subway stopped at the end of the J Line near Embassy Row, I had three solid suspects to tie in with Jeeves.

I worked a case once when I was with the cops. Some juvie dame busted into the cave of a couple of bears while the family was out for a walk in the woods. Kid stole some porridge -- and this was back during the Porridge Crisis when the stuff was importing for over a hundred bucks a barrel. This chick was so brazen she even took a nap in each one of the bears' beds. Beats me why she bed-hopped, and we never had the chance to question her. When the bears got back home and found the intruder, Papa Bear blew her to kingdom come with the rifle he kept over the fireplace. B & E, porridge theft, bed-napping. All causes for justifiable homicide. The bear got off clean. The NRA even ran an Armed Citizen piece applauding his actions defending his cave a few magazine issues later. The moral of the story was that people, like bears, would kill for a lot less than a golden throne, a bunch of palaces, power, butlers, serfs, colonies up the wazoo, and a couple of warehouses filled with royal jewels.

The three Albion princes were suddenly prime suspects, which made my problem particularly tricky. According to Merlin's note, if the "Queen" (magical bastard) had left town safe and sound, I would have been in the clear. Now that she'd been unmasked as a robot, the only way I could break the Pimlico Ruby curse was to save the Albion monarchy. And that wouldn't be simple. The only way I could do that might involve exposing one of the princes as the mastermind behind a plot that had resulted in two deaths as well as revelation of the Queen as a phony and a killer robot. That by itself would probably cause the monarchy to collapse, which meant that no matter what I did I was probably looking at a full-body appendectomy some time next week.

There were tons of news vans, local cop cars and Feds in sedans clogging the street in front of the Albion Embassy. A crowd had gathered holding signs with painted gems like "Robot Go Home!" and "Mean Queen

Machine!" *Jeopardy!* doesn't scrape up many contestants from your average sidewalk mobs.

There are times when a P.I. has to sneak over a back wall when nobody's looking and there are times when he shoves his way through a bunch of cops and a multitude of halfwits with signs to ring the front doorbell. With my bank account at immediate risk and the rest of my stuff soon to follow, this was no time for stealth.

I pushed my way through the crowd and yanked the tail of the royal lion. The roar on the other side of the wall was followed by a ruddy beefeater's face at the gates.

"I am authorized by 'Er Majesty's government to direct all inquiries to the embassy press office," the guard said, obviously repeating by rote his little speech for the millionth time that day. "You will find the number in your telephone directory. You will find when you call that number that it 'as been disconnected. Please get the message and kindly sod off and die. F'ank you very much, suh."

"I want to see Jeeves," I said before he could spin back around to take refuge in his booth. "The main Jeeves. The High Whizboom for Her Majesty's External Matters."

"Mr. Jeeves is in conference and cannot be disturbed," the guard informed me.

"Fine with me," I said. "Tell his royal pain-in-the-ass that I'll be holding an impromptu press conference out here in three minutes to let the world know exactly what his role in this is. Also, mention something to him about his prince-of-an-employer. Get that part especially right for old Cue-ball Jeeves." I immediately thought better of my choice of words. I'm no good at playing coy. "Ah, hell, just tell the plucked bastard that Banyon's here and if he doesn't see me I'm going to dump all the royal dirty laundry I know out on the sidewalk for these press vultures to pick through."

A minute after the guard entered his booth, the gates creaked open barely six inches. I had to squeeze through, and a bunch more beefeaters appeared at the entrance to shove back everybody who tried to cram in after me. I heard the gate lock behind me.

A butler in a penguin suit met me at the door and ushered me through a large hallway to a downstairs conference room.

Jeeves sat at the head of a gleaming table. Two rows of wheezing Albionmen were lined up like sweating bowling pins on either side of the table. I recognized the nearest on the left as the fat guy who'd gone nutso in the street after the fire plug burst and soaked the royal slipper the previous day.

The fat Albionman had a small metal box in front of him on the table, only as big as a deck of cards. The top had been unscrewed and the small screws and screwdriver sat beside it. He was poking around inside the box with two straight pins.

"Mr. Banyon," Jeeves announced. "I commend your tenacity. You seem genetically incapable of simply letting things go."

"I commend your scalp," I replied. "It seems genetically incapable of growing hair. Is that the liquor cabinet?"

It was. I poured myself whatever was in the nearest bottle and left the door to the ebony cabinet open as I took the seat at the head of the table opposite Jeeves.

The Albion high muckety-muck slowly retook his seat. "The gate said something about..." He waved his hand in the air, the very picture of innocent confusion. "The prince, was it? None of our highnesses are with us, lamentably. They are all back home attending to their dear mother." A flat stare and a twitch of a superior smile.

You can tell a lot from an asshole's twitch. So the real Queen was still alive.

"Let's cut through the crap, Jeeves. You blackmailed the demon into throwing that flying buttress at the robot. You even used the robot itself to order him to do it. You just stuffed her in a hood and probably used a remote speaker to give the order yourself right from the Robo-Queen's own mouth. Nice twist there. Real elegant-like. When that scheme fell flat on its ass thanks to me, you arranged for the alligators to open that hydrant at just the right spot on the parade route. Dollars to doughnuts you promised King Chompy something like official recognition from the Albion government. Mutant gators'll believe any lie. Whatever you told him can be found out easy enough. Cops can just send down Jack Hanna and a court stenographer in a cage."

I kept an eye peeled on the rest of the clowns around the table.

I saw lots of confusion, hesitation and bad teeth. Not one of the other Albions was racing to back Jeeves up.

"So I take it all of you knew about the Robot Queen," I said, "but none of you knew that old Jeeves here was the one trying to unmask it."

"Preposterous," Jeeves spluttered.

But halfway down the table, one old coot with a mustache longer than the *Complete Works of William Shakespeare Meets Dr. Who* raised a finger. It wasn't the finger I would've chosen to direct at Jeeves, but it still got everybody's attention.

"I say," the old codger said, "that...that...that hairy business in Mexico when Quetzalcoatl grabbed Her Robot Majesty while she was touring the floating gardens and dropped her into Popocatepetl volcano. Hell of a time explaining that one away to the press. You...you...you were there, old boy, weren't you?"

Another guy snapped his fingers. "And when she was touring the robot factory in Japan and that robot stuck that sticker that said 'I am a robot' in Japanese on her Royal Robotic Majesty's back. Why, you were on that diplomatic visit as well, Jeeves."

"Well, I would be, wouldn't I?" Jeeves snapped. "I *am* the High Whizboom for Her Majesty's External Matters."

I probably wasn't the only one who noticed he'd started to sweat.

"Well, yes, of course, but still," said the old coot. "Won't harm us to hear the fellow out." He glanced down the table at me. "Cat out of the bag, and all. It's no secret now that we've been deploying the robot for certain official duties of our flesh-and-blood Majesty. Harmless stuff. Secret of the Crown. Won't say more."

"You don't have to," I said. "It's all here in the Queen's official bio." I slapped down on the table the book Merlin had left at my office. "She made it clear a hundred and fifty years ago that she was determined to live forever to prevent her kids from ever taking over as king. I'm guessing one of them decided a sesquicentennial of waiting was long enough. Beats me which one of the bastards it was, and it doesn't matter. If it was the firstborn, he'd take her out then take the throne. If it was the last, he'd take her out then take out his brothers. Whichever one it is, he got Jeeves here in on the act. His instructions were make it so the Robo-Queen was exposed in order to embarrass the real one. All Albion would go nuts when it found out they'd been waving at a robot in a slipper coming out of the gates of Monmouth Palace for God knows how long. Public outcry would force the old gal to abdicate and one of her kids would eventually be sitting pretty on the throne. How much you want to bet that Jeeves has a real cushy gig lined up as soon the kid assumes the throne? All that sound about right to you, Jeeves?"

I once saw some egghead on TV talking about animals having two options when they're cornered: fight or flight. The first is hard on the knuckles, the last is hell on shoe leather. Personally, when I'm the guy doing the cornering I don't like the effort you've got to put into either option. That's why I prefer it when the rats I've cornered choose the German High Command option: unconditional surrender.

For a minute, I thought Jeeves would make the smart move and pick door number three. The conference room door was smack-dab behind me and, let's face it, the day I can't take some bloated old Albionman with skin the color of bleached bed sheets is the day I retire to a grass hut in the South Seas and spend the rest of my days picking off crabs with my .38. (Little sideways-running SOBs.)

"By Jove, I think that's got it," the fat man who'd been bawling in the middle of the street the previous day announced suddenly.

He was the only one in the room who hadn't been paying attention. I'd noticed, because even though I'd been particularly fascinating with my presentation, he'd kept on fiddling around with the two pins inside the little silver box. The pins were on the table at that moment, and he had just finished tightening the last screw into the back of the box.

Jeeves the cornered rat looked from me to the box in the fat man's hands. He glanced up once fast, exultant desperation on his sweaty face, and dove for the box.

And in that moment I knew exactly what that box was and why he was so suddenly desperate to get his hands on it. There was no way I could let that happen.

I jumped to slide dramatically down the length of the gleaming conference table in order to snatch up the little box before Jeeves could get his mitts on it. Hell, it always works in the movies. But real life isn't the movies, and all I managed was a spectacular belly-flop at the table's far end and a slide of about six inches. Either my $35 Sears suit wasn't conducive to dramatic table sliding, or the Albion Embassy's downstairs maid spent her whole day in the closet huffing all the liquid Pledge. Either way, when I looked up, Jeeves had backed far away from the table to the window.

The Queen's righthand traitor was poking desperately at the silver box in his hand. "You have no idea what you're talking about, Banyon!" he bellowed.

That's generally true. But I wasn't interested in talking at that moment. Unfortunately, by the time I was able to pull out my roscoe it was already too late.

I heard the whoosh closing in fast from somewhere outside the embassy's front wall. In front of every seated Albionman was a teacup and saucer that I'd failed to knock to the floor when I jumped on the table. All the fine China started rattling in place, as if the cups were being held by the arthritic old dames at the St. Regent's Octogenarian Ladies with Palsy Finger Sandwiches Social Club.

Just before the whoosh reached a crescendo and just as the shadow appeared in the window, I managed to squeeze off one shot.

I'm not exactly Robin Hood, the freak armored car thief on the FBI's most wanted list who'd been prancing around with a bunch of other bandits in green tights in the woods out in Montana. According to *USA Today*, that guy's such an expert sharpshooter he can split his first bullet in half with a second round. He never really shoots anyone he's aiming at, mostly because his bullets are always pinging off of one another and getting lodged in innocent bystanders. But it makes for a hell of a show for your average armored car driver outside the Safeway. As for me, I leave the trick shooting to the Wild West Show. I prefer a clean chest shot since that has the best chance of rendering my opponent the most dead. But in this case I was aiming for the box in Jeeves' hand, and I was as shocked as anyone when I managed to blast it.

The bullet slapped the side of the box and the little silver square spiraled out of Jeeves' hand. He fumbled to grab it, but wound up slapping it away with the backs of his fingers. It smacked against the wall and clattered to the floor under the window. The bald bastard dove to recover it just as the shadow outside loomed large over the floor-to-ceiling drapes, the whooshing became a bee-swarm hum in all our eardrums and the window exploded into the room in a million scattering shards of glass.

The curtains shredded and tore away from the snapped rod. Glass blasted across the conference table. Jeeves cowered under the window with his hands over his head as the rocket-powered figure flew straight over him and into the room.

The Robot Queen took a trip around the chandelier, circling the high ceiling once before coming in for a landing next to the broken window.

"*We are Albion! We enjoy sport!*"

Her mouth didn't move when she spoke. The Robo-Queen was still water damaged. The box they'd been working on must have been some kind of emergency remote control, but it hadn't overridden all the problems the busted hydrant had caused the inner workings of Her Royal Robotic Broadship.

I realized just how damaged the Robot Queen was when she picked up one of her royal staff and planted him noggin-first deep into the wall.

"We are Albion! We stage elaborate costume dramas which air without end on American public television!" the Robot Queen bellowed as she crushed the skull of another man between her small palms.

"I say!" cried the old man with the long mustache. He didn't say much after that, mostly since the Robot Queen tied the ends of his mustache so tight around his scrawny neck that his head came off in her hands.

I hadn't seen so much pandemonium and bloodshed in a fancy-ass conference room since I sat down with my ex-wife and her lawyers to hash out alimony. As the Robot Queen began to methodically slaughter her way through every poor schmoe within mechanical arm's reach, the rest of the room was cramming the door and all trying to get out at once and having about as much success at it as they'd have shoving a watermelon through a garden hose.

"Kill them all, your Robotic Majesty!" Jeeves screamed. "Remember your programming! The secret must be maintained at all costs!"

The bastard had recovered the remote. It was nicked in one corner and I saw some twisted, multicolored wires sticking out of my bullet hole.

Jeeves scrambled up by the window, glass falling from the back of his jacket, and stabbed frantically at the remote control with one fat finger as he yelled encouragement to the Robot Queen.

I'd seen enough busted microwaves to know she didn't need encouragement. The remote had some kind of homing signal that brought her there, but she was still malfunctioning. The old robot dame was slaughtering on her own time, not on his.

I slipped off the conference table and took a few shots at the royal metal maniac.

The bullets bounced off and didn't seem to slow her down any as she picked up another unlucky Albionman who was trying to run away. His legs continued to pump desperately at the air as she raised him over her head and tore him into two large chunks.

"*We are Albion! Our husbands are most certainly mostly not all poofters!*" the Robot Queen roared.

I wouldn't have any luck stopping her on my own. Next selection on the menu. I turned the barrel of my heater on Jeeves.

"Get her to stop, Jeeves, or I'll blow that jaundiced smile of yours to the back of your melon head."

The twisted grin of triumph on his face collapsed. "You wouldn't, Banyon."

I would, but in his defense Jeeves didn't know me too well, so I figured a demonstration of my seriousness was in order. I showed him I meant business by shooting off his left ear. (Maybe I'm not such a crummy shot after all.)

"*Dastard!*" Jeeves wailed in shock, slapping his hand to the bloody side of his head where his ear was suddenly shredded worse than the tattered drapes that blew around his slouched shoulders. "*Uncouth, savage American dastard!*"

"Is somebody asking me to put out the ringing in his other ear?" I asked, taking aim at the other side of the bald buzzard's bastard head.

"Cease! Stop!" Jeeves blurted. With the thumb of his free hand he stabbed furiously at the remote control.

The Robot Queen was holding the Minister of Foreign Cows by one leg and had been in the process of banging him senseless on the conference room table. It took several tries from Jeeves with the remote control, but finally a little green light lit up on the remote's end and the Robot Queen froze. She dropped the minister into a pile of bruised pinstripes, then turned abruptly and marched over to join Jeeves at the window.

The side of the Albionman's head was a bubbling fountain of red even with his fat hand pressed hard over his ear-hole. "Why do you even care about any of this?" he cried.

"I don't. I just made the mistake of coming to work on a Monday. Toss the remote down the table."

I like a scumbag who knows when he's been beat. Jeeves did as he was told. Unfortunately for me, when the remote hit the table, the side with the bullet hole cracked wide open and the electronic guts spilled out. All the lights at the top lit up at once, then snapped out, and suddenly the Robot Queen's hands were retreating up her forearms and an instant later her flamethrowers made an appearance nearly as unwelcome as Whoopi Goldberg from a giant stag party novelty cake.

"*We are Albion! We are not amused!*" the robo-Queen bellowed.

I wasn't exactly splitting my sides from laughing either as I turned and dove out the door. I felt the surge of heat at my back as I landed on the hallway floor and I rolled out of the path of the wall of flame that belched out behind me.

The stream of fire shot across the hall and lit up a painting of some ancient Albion king with a schnozz like Mr. Ed and a couple of naked angel babies flying around his crown. The painting and the wall around it went up like a booze-soaked bar rag.

I scrambled to my feet and tried to reload my gat as I flew down the hall. There was no way my bullets alone would make a difference. She shrugged off an army of cops the previous day. There was also no way I'd be able to outrun her if she was on my tail. One shot from her jetpack and she'd have me hoisted by my Fruit of the Looms.

They say that people on their deathbeds never wish they'd spent more time at work. That was sure as hell true for me. My wish was that I'd spent a lot more time away from work getting hammered. Specifically, the hour before I made the stupid decision to go to the Albion Embassy. To hell with the cursed ruby, being passed out drunk at O'Hale's at that moment was far preferable to getting roasted like a campfire marshmallow or turned into a human wishbone.

I'd just reached the main foyer and was racing for the door, surprised the Robot Queen hadn't blasted out into the hallway after me, when I heard a crash from back inside the conference room. I slid to a stop on a Persian welcome mat.

The Robo-Queen still wasn't coming out of the room. The fire on the wall with the big-nosed painting was spreading along the ceiling, and on the other side of the hall the doorframe to the conference room was burning kindling. But no Robot Queen.

No one ever gives me credit for having too much smarts. With the front exit and freedom wide open in front of me, I instead turned around and sprinted back into the burning building and up the hall to the conference room.

The Robo-Queen and Jeeves were still inside. Flames were chewing up the walls and racing across the thick beams.

The crash I'd heard was from the chandelier, which the fire had burned loose. It had fallen and split the conference table halfway up, and there were chunks of crystal scattered all over the burning carpet.

The Robot Queen wasn't coming after me because she already had her hands full. Jeeves was curled up in her arms like a sack of Albion potatoes. I was just in time to see her jetpack kick on. The rocket's flame joined the rest of the fire and burned a precision hole in the carpet as she blasted through the wall out into sunlight.

Too bad for Jeeves there's a big difference what a flying robot monarch with a metal chassis and a pudgy one-eared embassy dummy can take as far as the whole punching-through-walls department was concerned.

The robot flew up and out of sight. Ten seconds later, Jeeves fell back into view and landed pretty much like a sack of Albion potatoes in a tangle of rose bushes. I heard the whoosh of the jetpack as the Robot Queen took off for parts unknown.

I stepped as carefully as I could through the burning door and into the million-degree heat of the conference room. All the antique chairs around the table were in flames, each one of them worth more than what I took home in a year. Probably because Napoleon hadn't parked his ass on my twenty-two grand after taxes take-home income.

I found what I was looking for in a pile of crystal chandelier pieces surrounded by burning chunks of table. I quickly snatched up the busted remote control, stopped just long enough to heroically rescue a couple of innocent bottles from the liquor cabinet, and ran like a rabbit back out into the smoke-filled hallway.

Chapter 13

The only evidence of the fun-filled hijinks outside Polly Skidmore's Pawn Shop two nights before were a few busted bits of fenders and grilles as well as a ton of windshield glass that was scattered like pixie dust all around the street. Also there was the small matter of the BMW that was still wedged like a two thousand pound rectangle in a square hole in the mouth of the alley beside the building.

When I showed up, a tow truck crew was trying to figure out how pop the Kraut wreck loose. The Robot Queen had really done a number jamming the BMW in there good and tight. The three tow truck stooges were hooking a cable up under the remains of the right front tire well as I headed into the hock shop.

There had been police tape strung up at one point but most of it had been ripped down, pretty angrily by the looks of it. The tape was in a gnarled yellow pile of shreds on the floor inside the remains of the door. Only a few yellow knots remained on the twisted posts at the front of the store. The car that the Robo-Queen had launched inside Polly's had been dragged out and hauled away, but there were tread marks on the cheap tile floor and the dump reeked of gas. And not the usual you get from Polly after a week of him binge-eating nothing but grape soda and Taco Bell takeout.

All eight hundred pounds of Polly Skidmore was back behind what was left of the glass cases that he surrounded himself with and which he used as a counter, mostly to hold up Domino's Pizza boxes, two liter bottles of cream soda, and Polly's flabby, hairy arms. Most of the display cases had been busted apart and their contents had been stripped. Could've been by Polly himself cleaning up, by the cops doing some early Christmas shopping or by locals who descended on the place after Polly had been hauled off and locked up in stir. By the glare he gave me as I walked up to the counter, I'd be wise not to ask, so I made a conscious decision to be on my absolute best behavior.

"In my day, assaulting a cop with a voodoo doll automatically got a perp hauled off to Beggar's Island without a phone call, lawyer or bail," I said, flashing a disarming grin. "Congratulations, Polly, for being such a fat-ass they were afraid you'd sink the prison ferry if they rolled you on it." (I'm so sweet I could get a job writing Hallmarks.)

"What do you want, Banyon?" Polly demanded. "You know, I'm holding you responsible for everything what happened here. You's gettin' a bill, buddy boy."

"You could send one," I said. "Of course, I'll just feed it through my office shredder, assuming you have a shredder I can pick up for cheap lying around in the ruins of your livelihood. We can negotiate that in a minute. In the meantime, if you want to shake down somebody who you've got an actual shot of getting paid by, you'd be better off sending that bill to Her Royal Robot Highness, care of Monmouth Palace."

Polly put down the bag from which he'd just taken a handful of Extra-Salty Caramel Bugles. "What do you mean?" he said as he chewed with his mouth wide open which, if I'd had a camera to record it, I could have sold for a bundle to Jenny Craig as an overeaters scared-straight video.

"I mean that robot dame in the crown all over the news is the one that booked double duty the other night remodeling your joint. She's not much for valet parking, but she makes up for it with that famous Albion pluck."

Polly's piggy eyes narrowed. "Cops said you told them you didn't know who it was."

"Didn't then. Do now. The genius local constabulary probably don't know yet because Jenkins is no doubt leading the investigation with his usual finesse, that of a tone-deaf orchestra conductor with his baton up his ass. But it'll be easy to prove." I offered him my most honest shrug. "If you try to stick me with the tab for this, Polly, you're screwed. I'm fifty percent more broke today than I was yesterday and tomorrow is shaping up to be just as counterproductive. On the other hand, the Albion royal family has more money than God, at least according to that *60 Minutes* investigation where they dug up His tax info from a trash barrel behind the Vatican, so if you really want to get paid for this party, that's the money tree you want to be shaking."

Polly grunted. "Say for a minute I believe you. I know you, Banyon. You didn't come down here to do me no favors. Whaddaya want from me?"

I fished in my pocket and handed over the Robot Queen's busted remote control. "First, can you fix this?"

Polly was a whale, yeah, but he was a cetacean with delicate flippers. The electronic junk that got dumped off at Polly Skidmore's Pawn Shop got cleaned up real nice and usually sold for a hefty profit. It was still cheaper than Best Buy, and if something you bought there broke on the way out the door you had Polly's unconditional guarantee that he would take it off your hands at half the price you paid for it two minutes before and resell it at double the price to the next sucker who walked through the door.

Polly slipped on a pair of Shamu-size bifocals and took a long look at the remote.

"Yeah, probably fixable. Course you won't know if it really works if you don't have the robot it goes to nearby to test it out on," he added, looking up at me over the tops of his bifocals.

So he knew it wasn't to my lava lamp. No surprise there. There were never any flies on Polly. Not since he switched from Right Guard to Black Flag.

Polly pulled off his glasses. "Okay, that's first. What else you want?"

I flashed him my most disarming smile. "I need to borrow one of your more expensive pieces of equipment. You know. From the special stuff in the basement that hasn't been driven over like the crap up here."

His angry eyelids squeezed so tight over his jaundiced eyes I figured they might burst and shower me with Mountain Dew.

"Hey," I shrugged, "you've got to spend money to make it, Polly. Of course, I only understand that in the abstract since I've never done either."

# # #

I called the office from a payphone around the corner from Polly Skidmore's Pawn Shop. Mannix picked up before the first ring finished.

"Hey, Mannix. You get to the hospital like I asked?" "Yes, sir, Mr. Crag. It wasn't easy. There were guards there, police and other men. Your friend Detective Jenkins was there."

"Did he see you?"

"No. I was going to say hello, but I remembered that you didn't want anyone to see me, so I didn't."

"Good. I don't want you talking to any bastards while you're on the clock unless they're me. Did you get what I wanted?"

"Yes, sir," the elf said.

"Okay, I want you to take that and the photos I had you collect from the papers and get over to Halloween and Party Supplies over on 17th. Madame Arugula's the dame who runs the joint. She owes me for exorcising a batch of haunted Power Rangers costumes a couple years back. Goddamned ghosts. Tell her we're square if she does exactly what I told you. But she's got to work fast. You got all that?"

"Yes, sir, Mr. Crag."

"When you're done, get back to the office and sit by the phone in case I need you for anything else. But probably you'll be able to cool your heels for a few hours since I'm going to be out of the game for a little while, so play some rummy with the mice or something. Just don't open the door for anyone. Jenkins will probably be stopping by there after the disappearing act I pulled at the embassy. Lock the door and stay huddled in there until I need you. You don't like to lie -- which, incidentally, I find to be very irritating -- so it's better you don't see him. Anyway, he'd just strut around demanding I don't leave town like he always does, and who needs those headaches, especially when I never leave town?"

"Okay," Mannix said. "But where will you be?"

"Booking a flight out of the country."

Chapter 14

"This is your captain speaking. We are beginning our descent to Vauxhall and Churchbatton Airport. Please return your trays to their folded and upright positions. If there are any firestarters onboard, kindly refrain from any pyrokinetic displays until after the plane has completed taxiing to the terminal. Thank you, passengers, and thank you once again for flying Albion Airlines. God save the Queen."

The speakers cut out in static, but a moment later the pilot came back on.

"The *human* Queen," he amended.

The pilot sounded as annoyed as pretty much every Albionman I'd heard blabbing on the flight over. Nobody was happy that they'd been shoveling hard-earned tax dollars into their beloved, bejeweled Queen's bank account only for her to send out a collection of wires and computer chips to take her place while she kicked back at her summer palace in Ibiza. Assuming she was even alive. Jeeves seemed to indicate she was, but for some reason the real Queen had yet to stick her crowned head out the front door of Monmouth Palace to assure her subjects that she was still God's #1 choice to run the joint.

I felt the change in pressure in my ears as the plane nosed down. I'm not a big fan of flying, but only because they don't allow the stewardesses to give you enough booze to get you really good and hammered anymore, all thanks to some obnoxious Gorgon who got so pounded on a Russian Air flight last year that she yanked off her mandatory bag and turned half the flight crew and everyone in first class to stone after she found out the in-flight movie was *Transformers II*. Like she wouldn't have done the exact same thing stone-cold sober. But because of her I was forced to arrive dry in the Albion capital.

I checked my wallet as I deplaned. Last time I looked I still had the twenty-five bucks from Merlin, but it had halved itself again and was down to $12.50.

"Wizard son of a bitch," I said.

I didn't realize I'd said it out loud until a ton of airport security came out of the woodwork and piled on a wizard in a stars-and-moon business suit behind me. The guy must've overheard me and was in the middle of an offended incantation with his hands raised and a little lightning-spitting thundercloud forming above his head. The magic cloud dissipated as soon as the white-shirts tackled him, and they were slapping on the cuffs as I beat a hasty retreat out the sliding glass doors into a country of fog and rain.

You go to Vauxhaull, you expect lousy weather, so that was true to form.

Through the sheets of driving rain, the whole place still looked like a typical Albion postcard. I'm not a big fan of postcards, mostly because my mailbox usually pukes out about a hundred of the things whenever Doris is on vacation. Every time she's gone I have to haul an empty trash barrel downstairs just to deal with the extra mail, and then when she gets back I have to lie and tell her they were all my favorites and that I didn't keep any around the office because I had them all taped in my postcard scrapbook under my pillow at home. Nice kid. Stupid as hell.

Negotiating through the Albion capital was like spinning the postcard rack at the airport apothecary's. No matter where the wheel landed, there was another famous, clichéd landmark staring me in the face. On the way to the hotel I passed Vauxhall Bridge, Cow Tower, The Tricarmel Legislation House, the mile-high Statue of Lord Smedlington and Plague Square. Starving peasant kids in rags begged for duodenums on every street corner. From the top of my triple-decker orange bus I spotted about a hundred dead donkeys dumped all along the sides of the streets.

Far above the city, chimney sweeps danced on rooftops and hacked so much black phlegm over the sides that the sidewalks looked liked flattened Dalmatians.

The bus dumped me at the Vauxhall Royal Hotel. When I stepped down to the street all I could smell was wet hay, horse crap, beer, vomit and fish and chips.

In the lobby, a kid in a red bellboy outfit was chasing a goat into the waiting arms of a white-clad chef. The chef gathered the goat up and hauled it off to the kitchen for that evening's main course of blood-and-hookworm pie.

I'd seen on the million TV screens in the airport terminal that the protests were still going on outside Monmouth Palace. It was a pretty typical European mob, loaded down with the standard pitchforks and torches. There were also a lot of scythes, which wasn't a surprise. Scything was the third biggest industry in Albion after roof thatching and knickers stitching.

I'd picked up a disposable cell phone before leaving home and used it once to call Mannix before the plane landed. The phone happened at that moment to ring once and only once, then went dead in my pocket. Perfect timing.

I called the bellboy over as I checked in.

"Hey, kid, run something over to the palace for me." I fished in my trench coat pocket and held up an envelope. "When you're through there, run to the hardware store and pick me up two scythes and a pitchfork, and get them back here pronto."

He held out his hand for a tip. I slapped the envelope in it and told him they'd take care of him at the palace.

My bed was a crushed hay stack in the corner of my room and my bathroom was a communal phone booth at the end of the hall with a European ass fountain and a tub barely big enough to drown a cat in. I knew this to be true, since the maid was in the process of trying to do just that when I went in to powder my nose.

"'Ere, 'e's a righ' ol' feisty tabby, in't 'e, guv'nah?" she asked, flashing a jack-o'-lantern smile while the feline she was baptizing howled and scratched.

I powdered my nose off the nearest balcony.

From my hotel window I could see the glow of the mob parked outside the main gates of Monmouth Palace.

Albion's had been a fairly stable political system since the Queen took over in the late 1700s. By the looks of it that day, stability could change course on a dime. The crowds were growing bigger and madder every day the Queen didn't make an appearance. It wouldn't take much of a push to get them to bust through the gates and do a Louis XVI number on the whole royal family. And the guillotine wouldn't stop with them. Thanks to Merlin and his cursed ruby, if I didn't figure out a way to save the royal inbreds, it'd keep chopping until it diced up everything I owned, including me.

The bellboy returned an hour later with an armload of gardening equipment and a message from the palace.

"They will be sending a coach round for you in one hour, Mr. Banyon."

He leaned the scythes and pitchfork against the cow in the corner of my room and headed for the door without another word.

"Just like that? No questions?"

"None, sir."

"They tipped you all right at the palace?" I asked as he was closing the door.

"Oh, *yes*, sir," the kid said, and when he flashed a smile I knew the fine people at Colgate would never see a penny of it.

It figured. The errand boy gets rich and I was stuck with a curse, a shrinking bank account and a mental image of a set of putrid dog teeth that'd haunt me forever.

The coach showed up right on schedule an hour later. The gas lights along all the streets were just flickering on. The streetlights seemed to possess some supernatural power that drew from the shadows buzzing flies, sloppy hookers and staggering drunks.

The coachman braved the drizzle to open the door for me, and wasn't put off in the least when I had him load up the gardening tools in the back of the pumpkin; he just accepted them with the quiet, dignified subservience that the great servant class of Albion famously displayed right up until they murdered everyone in the manor in their sleep or sold Lady Penelope's dirty underwear to the *Sun*.

I took my seat on the cushioned bench in the back. I could see the driver shake out the reins through the slit cut in the front of the pumpkin. The pair of white horses took off through the cobbled, hay-covered streets of Vauxhall.

I heard the angry crowd as we closed in on the palace. The weird glow from thousands of torches splashed wild shadows across both the tall glass modern buildings and the many squat blacksmith shops with anvils and tinkers' horses parallel parked out front. The driver steered the coach along streets at the edge of the crowd. At one point we strayed a little too close and someone sank a pitchfork into the side of the pumpkin near my ankle. The coachman whipped the horses and the three pitchfork tines quickly slipped back out as the carriage sped away from the mob.

The bulk of the crowd was massed near the main gates of the palace. My driver took the long way around, down a private bridge across the river and through a secret tunnel that fed into the back grounds of Monmouth Palace. The horses clopped up to a quiet side entrance where another servant in a high powdered wig helped me down.

"Mr. Banyon, sir," he droned, glancing past me at the tools inside the pumpkin. "You are expected. I will have your implements sent along. Please, walk this way."

I couldn't walk that way because, unlike him, I wasn't crammed inside a pair of ballerina tights and wooden high heels, so I made do with following him inside.

As palaces went, Monmouth was a pretty okay dump. The ceilings were so high I was pretty sure I saw clouds. You could fly a Cessna through the main hallway and land it in the drawing room where they parked me.

The room was at the front of the palace, and huge ceiling-to-floor drapes were drawn on the windows. Even so, the flickering glow of torches could be seen through the purple, gilded brocade and while the rumble from the multitude waiting out by the front curb was muted, it came through loud and clear enough for me.

The Albion sense of duty and loyalty was something to behold. None of the servants seemed flustered by what was going on just outside the front gates. The butler who brought in my gardening tools and leaned them on the arm of the couch might have been a windup toy like the Robot Queen Herself for all the interest he displayed in the insanity going on outside. If I'd been an eighth floor chambermaid I'd have been knotting royal bed sheets together and running like hell for France between the gandaberunda pond and the human chess board out back.

A minute after the butler had deposited me on a couch that looked like a silk-covered snail shell, a skinny guy with a pair of glasses stuck on the end of his nose and a gleaming leather satchel tucked up under his arm came into the room. If his business suit was any smarter it could've gotten early admission at Yale. He had the sincere smile of a particularly crooked used car dealer.

"Hello, Mr. Banyon. I am Hastings. I represent Her Majesty's government."

He offered me his hand. I've wrung out firmer wet socks.

"We received your packet with interest," Hastings informed me.

I could use more of his kind of interest. He pulled a binder from his satchel, flipped it open on the mahogany table before the couch and began writing a check.

"Mr. Merlin was, as you've no doubt ascertained, an eccentric individual," Hastings said as he wrote. "I read the copy of his contract with you which you sent along, as have the Queen's crackerjack palace lawyers. Unfortunately, according to the terms to which you unwittingly agreed, the Cursed Ruby of Pimlico will continue to halve your savings in perpetuity. Well, at least until the end of *you*. But there are ways around all curses, of course." He tore off the check and slid it across the table.

There'd been fewer zeroes at Pearl Harbor. Hastings offered an oily smile.

"A payoff isn't going to cut it," I said. I slid the check back.

The smile thinned. "You do realize that the palace doesn't have to offer you a thing," Hastings said. "A man of your--" He offered a flickering sneer as he sized up my wardrobe which, unlike everybody who worked at the royal armpit, didn't look like it had been mugged off the wine steward at the Albion Ritz. "Well, shall we say a man of your *meager* means cannot hope to hold out against the curse for very long."

"And that dough would barely get me through two weeks. You think your monarchy is going to last long enough to cut me a second check? As soon as the Queen falls, the monarchy fails and I'm done for. That was in Merlin's contract too."

"Yes," Hastings said. "I'm not quite sure what you expect from me, Mr. Banyon."

"I expect you to leave a trail of slime across that woven Indian carpet when you go off to tell the real Queen, wherever she's hiding, that I can save all this *and* my hide."

Hastings quietly closed up his fancy checkbook inside his fancy satchel and hauled his fancy ass back out the door.

They made me cool my jets another hour. Finally, a footman in a huge powdered wig and a pair of purple pantaloons appeared at the door and signaled me to follow.

The servant carried the two scythes and the pitchfork onto a small elevator at the end of a gloomy hallway. Inside smelled like a cedar coffin.

The elevator doors opened on a corridor lined with white plastic walls. Florescent lights hummed behind panels that were covered in thick sheets of translucent plastic.

The one door was at the far end of the hallway, and near the end we had to pass through a plastic gate like the metal detectors at your finer inner city American public schools. The footman had me pause while I was bathed in a weird red light. The light switched off, a bulb glowed green on the white plastic wall, and a mechanized voice announced, "Scan complete. Please wipe your feet."

The door at the end of the hall led into a large chamber. I got the sense that it was round, although I couldn't make out the walls in the gloom. Bright lights were arranged on stands at the center of the room where a glass sarcophagus was propped up on what looked like a five foot long, four foot high solid gold block.

Inside the transparent box lay the Queen of Albion.

She looked pretty much like her robot stand-in. Maybe a little older, with a few more wrinkles and whiter hair. But for an old dame of 236, she looked pretty okay.

A dozen chairs were lined up before the box, but only three were occupied. Thanks to Ed Jaublowski and the TV at O'Hale's, I recognized the three Albion princes. The Queen's three elderly sons were poking each other in the ribs, grousing, laughing inappropriately and pointing into the shadows at things that probably weren't there. They weren't the least interested in me or in their mother lying in the sarcophagus.

Hastings and several other nervous men in suits stood next to the box. I noticed one face in particular half-hidden at the back with a couple of beefeater guards.

At first I thought the Queen was dead, but when I got close, she turned sharp eyes on me.

"Hello, Mr. Banyon," the Queen of Albion said.

What do you say to a broad who's been running a world power for over two centuries? Beats me. All I know is I'm more impressed with Duke Ellington, Erle Stanley Gardner and the Burger King than I am with real royalty. Those guys actually earned whatever they made with every toot, typewriter tap or french fry, and they sure as hell didn't have a scepter handed to them in a box of Cracker Jacks as a reward for dropping their first torpedo in the royal commode.

"Hey, sweetheart," I said. "Hot enough for you?"

It was about a million degrees inside the circle of lamps. I noted the puddles on the floor. The inside of the sarcophagus was fogged with dew that burned off in the heat only to quickly reform and steam away again. The whole room stunk like my apartment the one and only time Doris defrosted my freezer and found a decayed orc head frozen in the back. (*That* had been a crazy case.)

"As we understand it," the Queen announced, "now that the world has learned of the Royal Robot, there has been much speculation that we are dead. You, however, seem not surprised that we are alive."

I shrugged. "Jeeves accidentally let the cat out of the bag when he said the princes were back here watching you."

"Ah, Jeeves. We are gravely disappointed in him."

"I'm gravely disappointed the son of bitch will pull through. He's in the hospital back home. I was hoping your robot would've killed him when she dropped him as they were making their getaway. You know she nearly burned down your embassy? I hope you kept the receipt or at least got one of those extended robot warranties."

"Indeed. Help us up."

"Lady, you must have got an F in math, because according to my count right now there's only one of you. But if you point me to the nearest pub after we've concluded our business I can remedy that in short order."

The Queen pushed herself to a sitting position. There were hooks on my side of the sarcophagus. Hastings and the other men made a move for them, but the Queen froze them with a glare. I undid the hooks, the side of the glass box flipped open, and the Queen swung her legs over the side. I helped her to the floor.

She was short, her arm was cold and her skin was tinged blue.

"How long have you been asleep?" I asked.

"Off and on for the past seventy years," the Queen said. "We are thawed for important occasions. Mostly our robot exercises our duties while we keep track of world events with a cybernetic implant that feeds data directly into our cerebral cortex."

"I usually just turn on the radio. My ice bill's already through the roof."

"Mumsy!" a voice shouted from across the room.

When he saw his mother was up and about, Prince Gormless clomped over, shoving his teeth and a crayon drawing in the Queen's face.

"Mumsy, I saved a tree!" the prince shouted.

At least I think that's what he said. The royal choppers were an impediment even before private tutors had gotten hold of him and given him an accent that made it sound like his tongue had been fed through a pasta maker. It sounded to my uncouth ear like, "Mmsyissffedatwee." Lucky for me, he had the visual aid.

The picture he'd drawn was of himself sitting on top of a leafy green tree. A crying man sat in a bulldozer below. The prince wore a big yellow crown. A smiling squirrel sat in the treetop beside him. Unlike the real-life prince, the guy in the drawing didn't have gray hair, liver spots and arthritis. The prince in the drawing was young and virile as he and his squirrel pal stared into the smiling face of the yellow sun.

The Queen patted her 164 year old eldest son on the top of the head.

"How lovely, dear. Go play with your brothers."

Prince Gormless galloped on awkward, gangly legs to rejoin his siblings.

"I can see why they had to thaw you the modern way," I said. "There is certainly a paucity of handsome princes to smack a queen awake around this dump."

"Do you have children, Mr. Banyon?" the Queen asked, sighing heavily.

"Not that any of the paternity tests could prove."

"Then you cannot know the great disappointment we have felt." The old dame shook her head. "We have three idiot children, Mr. Banyon, not one suited to assume the throne after us. We have been forced to freeze ourselves and send a robot out in our stead so that we might prolong our reign. There. Look. Those are the princes of Albion, over there in that corner wrestling over what we think is a Batman comic book. Boys, stop that! Your sovereign mother the Queen demands that you stop giving one another Red Indian sunburns this instant. We will not pay for another hip replacement!"

"Sorry, mumsy," the sheepish elderly princes replied in unison.

"The burden we have had to endure, Mr. Banyon," the Queen said wearily, "is greater than you can possibly comprehend."

The Queen began to walk and beckoned that I come along. I felt the mass of men huddled in the shadows around the sarcophagus trailing behind us.

"Jeeves wasn't plotting with any of them, was he," I said.

She sighed. "Would that they were capable of plotting. No, Mr. Banyon, he was acting on his own. We had been receiving blackmail letters, we knew not from whom. We did not pay, so he clearly sought to unmask our robot as an act of vengeance. We thank you for your help in flushing out Jeeves. He will be dealt with."

"Hey, the tip jar is always out on the counter."

She ignored me. I guessed she hadn't become one of the richest women on the planet by giving well-earned gratuities to the hardworking help. She'd become one of the richest women on the planet by being the daughter of one of the richest men on the planet and sitting on the interest of her inherited loot for two centuries. Nice work if you can get it.

"We have had our advisors tell us that you believe you can save our kingdom," the Queen said as she passed through a side door into a paneled corridor. "It is unfortunate that Merlin brought you into this business. He had our best interests at heart, and wanted only to root out whomever was behind the attempts to unmask before the world our robot doppelganger. He gave you one of his cursed diamonds, we gather."

"Ruby," I said.

"Oh," she said, packing a boatload of disdain into the syllable. "You are, Mr. Banyon, as our American cousins say, a cheap date. In any event, we appreciate your kind offer, but it is unnecessary. These events shall pass."

"Lady, you just woke up so let me tell you what's going on outside. You've got an army of royally pissed-off taxpayers in the front yard demanding your crown on a pike, and from what I can see they'll be more than happy to burn this place and half the city to the ground on their way back out the door. A cheery hello and one of your patented windshield-wiper waves from a fiftieth floor balcony isn't going to cut it this time. Now personally, I would ordinarily not give a crap. At this time of day, my greatest concern is usually a half-empty glass of antifreeze and counting the hairs on the legs of the dead flies in the peanut bowl at my corner watering hole. But thanks to your court wizard, I've been lassoed into this mess, so I'd appreciate it if you treated it like the end of the world it is for all of us."

"We cannot share your worries," the Queen said. "You are, to be blunt, Mr. Banyon, an insignificant individual. We are not. We have lived a great many years. We shall live a great many more as Queen. Our subjects are children who must be led and, lamentably, our children are subjects best left undiscussed."

"Okay, you haven't a clue that the Sword of Damocles is about to drop on this royal racket of yours," I said. "No surprise you'd be out of touch, what with the palaces and jewelry and those frolicking harlequins staging a one-act French farce over in that glass case in the corner. Let's try another tack. I spill everything I know about this to the press. So I get sliced in half when the curse kicks in. I'll at least get the pleasure of seeing you go first."

We had just entered another large chamber. The Queen turned and gave me a look of pitying condescension.

"We are going nowhere," she said. "You, on the other hand, Mr. Banyon..."

She turned the old-fashioned crank light switch on the wall. Torches flared to life along ancient brick walls.

She'd led me to a dungeon. In the middle of the room a towering figure in a black hood stood leaning on the handle of a very large ax next to a chopping block and a stained wicker basket.

"I didn't realize you had an appointment with the royal hair stylist," I said. "Why don't I just take a seat out in the waiting room? Tell him not so thick with the polyurethane this time. He's going to have to jackhammer that tiara loose."

I didn't get the chance to take more than three steps back.

"Guards!" the Queen shouted

She adjusted her handbag on her forearm as a pair of beefeaters who'd been following our group hustled forward and grabbed my arms, pinning them behind me.

The Queen circled around before me.

"We did not survive this long to be undone at this late date," she insisted. "You cannot appreciate the intricacies involved in maintaining our deceit. A small man like you could not comprehend the tiniest detail that has vexed our royal personage, right down to something as seemingly trivial as mouse dispersal."

Just like that, I suddenly had something in this that interested me more than me getting hacked into little Banyon bits.

"What do you mean, mouse dispersal?" I asked, narrowing my eyes.

"Have you ever had mice nest in your motorized carriage, Mr. Banyon? I am told they are a great nuisance, chewing through wires and building smelly little nests inside those fiddly little inner workings that make all machinery go. The Royal Robot is no different. When we first deployed her on a trip to Malaysia, some local vermin which did not grasp the great majesty of our duplicate climbed into her head and chewed through most of the wires therein. She went berserk and wiped out an entire sweater factory. Bits of yellow angora were raining down on Kuala Lumpur for days after the massacre. We had a devil of a time keeping that out of the press. Ever since, before all of our visits, we have sent a radiophonic device that scatters to the four winds any mouse within the area she will be visiting. It works on some supersonic wavelength that only mice can hear. We do not understand the technology, we only know that it has worked for decades to remove the mouse problem."

"It doesn't remove it, lady, it just makes it somebody else's problem."

She offered an indifferent little wave. "Somebody else's problem is not our problem," the goddamned Queen of goddamned Albion goddamned announced goddamned breezily.

If I'd had on me at that moment one of the mice that had been terrorizing my poor defenseless booze back home, I would have stuck it in the royal ear and seen what kind of damage it could do chewing through the royal ratbag's cybernetic implant.

The Queen continued, oblivious to everything beyond the end of the royal conk.

"The mob outside shall be quelled," Her Royal Pain-in-the-Assness said. "An explanation shall be made about the Royal Robot. It was only used a handful of times, or so

159

will go the official story. We were never frozen. The people will be satisfied. You, however, will not be alive to see any of it." She leaned in close and I got a full wallop of a decade of Albion morning breath and the lifetime lack of Scope that preceded it. "You really should have taken the money, Mr. Banyon."

After two centuries with her ample ass parked on Albion's gem-encrusted throne, I don't think the old bird was used to being surprised by much of anything, so I was pretty satisfied with myself when my blasé shrug merited a raised royal eyebrow. Even mild surprise from the Queen of Albion was probably more rare than a damp toothbrush around Monmouth Palace.

"I didn't get into this business to get rich," I said. "I got into it because I like looking in other people's windows. And you're forgetting one thing, Shorty. Jeeves. That bald bastard is still alive. You can kill me all you want, but he's got all the inside palace skinny on you and your robot, and right now he's in the hospital under the protection of the greatest cop who ever lived, Detective Daniel Jenkins."

A small, smug smirk crossed the royal kisser. "Quite," said the Queen.

She tipped her tiara ever-so-slightly and there was a sudden commotion at the rear of the crowd of palace hangers-on that had followed us into the dungeon. Two more guards came forward, propelling a short, bald figure before them.

Jeeves' face was devoid of any hint of emotion.

The Queen shook her head. "Regrettably for your sake, Mr. Banyon, our Jeeves turned himself in to us not long before your arrival. So you see, this *will* end here."

The old dame had lived such an insulated life, apparently seventy of those years packed away in actual insulation, that she truly thought this was the old days, when a scandal ended at the drop of an ax after which the Earl of Pudgedoodle could go happily back to molesting the local sheep without a care about peasants, press or PETA.

The guards propelled Jeeves toward the executioner.

"Our Jeeves has insisted that he go first," the Queen explained. "His latent sense of duty to his Queen and country has reasserted itself. I wonder, Mr. Banyon, if you will demonstrate such courage when it is your neck for the chop."

"Stop wondering. I call the paramedics when I cut my toenails."

Jeeves voluntarily got to his knees and placed his head on the chopping block. His head was leaning to one side, right cheek pressed to the old wooden block. He stared at the Queen with blank eyes. "I am ready, Majesty," Jeeves said.

"Just out of curiosity while I'm still in one piece," I asked. "Does the royal executioner see a lot of referrals from you?"

"Oh, you know, just some journos," the Queen said. "TV presenters who have displeased us. The occasional bishop."

She didn't look at me as she spoke. Her eyes were flat and trained on Jeeves and the man who was raising his ax high in the air behind the kneeling bald sucker.

Torchlight danced on the edge of the upright blade.

The ax fell and met the block with a thwack, and a split second later there came an accompanying soft thump inside the rattling basket.

The Queen curled her lip at me. "It is your turn on the block, Mr. Banyon."

It was clear when the old biddy turned to face me that she hadn't expected I'd be smiling right back at her. In two hundred years she probably hadn't seen much change in human behavior, so some jerk grinning on the way to his execution probably wasn't a common sight, Charles Dickens and *A Tale of Two Cities* be damned.

The royal yap opened, but before she could question me, a voice chimed in from across the room.

"*I am ready, Majesty.*"

The Queen and everyone else turned very slowly toward the executioner and the still-rattling wicker basket next to the chopping block.

"*I am ready, Majesty,*" the voice of Jeeves repeated from inside the basket.

The executioner reached into the basket and pulled out the head. Wires trailed from the neck. Jeeves' mouth was locked open and, although his lips and tongue didn't move, the words came out as clear as a bell one last time, "*I am ready, Majesty.*"

"That's a wrap, Mannix," I called.

There was a burst of static, the mouth on the decapitated head twitched, and the voice of my trusty assistant elf who doesn't get paid anywhere near enough, mainly because I so rarely pay him, chimed out of the head's mouth hole.

"Are you okay, Mr. Crag?" Mannix's voice asked.

"Head still attached, song still in my heart. Did you get everything?"

"I recorded everything from the moment the Robot Mr. Jeeves arrived at the palace," Mannix said. The head's eyes slid to the Queen and the brows twitched down at the center. "That was very, very, *very* naughty of you to try to cut off Mr. Crag's head," Mannix's voice scolded. "That's just about the naughtiest thing I ever heard. And I used to be in the naughty or nice business, so I know. Shame on you, Mrs. Queen."

Her Majesty the Royal Patsy wasn't even listening to the elf's admonishments coming out of the robot traitor's head. She turned to me, royal lips pursed like she'd just been told she'd lost three Caribbean islands and half of Africa to Belgium.

"You taped us?" the Queen said.

"Just-- Hey, one second, will you?"

I yanked my right arm free from the Beefeater Gin guard who was still pinning it behind my back and sent my elbow square back in his pasty face. He dropped to his knees, grabbing for his bloody, busted schnozz.

I spun around and sent a haymaker into the jaw of the second guard, who went sprawling to the floor. I know what a busted jaw sounds like -- giving and receiving -- so I knew that the cold-cocked beefeater, when he finally woke up, would be sipping his intestines through a straw for the next six weeks.

I turned back to the Queen, adjusting the cuffs of my trench coat. "Glass jawed bastard. Anyway, as I was saying, all we got was you saying your beloved subjects are idiot sheep, how your kids are morons, how you've been playing this cryogenic lie for seventy years, how you plan on lying to your subjects about how much you used the robot, and how you still chop off heads in your basement rec room. If you want, I can have my associate burn you a copy of your greatest hits. *After* he sends copies to every major news organization around the world, of course."

Everybody telegraphs when they've been beat. I don't care if it's some bum at the corner pool hall who never had a pot to piss in, or royalty born with a silver footman next to the toilet paper dispenser and gold-plated caviar in their mouths. You can see it in their eyes, shoulders, hands. Not that I needed the visual confirmation with this dame.

Her Royal Handbag, the Queen of Albion, released a deeply putrid sigh.

"What is it you desire, Mr. Banyon?" she asked, with regal reluctance.

"I've got an itemized list of desires right here," I said, patting my breast pocket.

I wasn't paying as much attention to the old bird as she was probably used to, mainly because I'd just heard a noise. It was a little later than I'd expected. The others in the dungeon heard the sound as well. The men looked up as all around us the walls of the palace began to shake as if an earthquake had just hit downtown Vauxhall.

The whooshing sound grew louder, itching my eardrums. Some of the others clapped their hands over their ears. The sound reached a crescendo, the wall suddenly collapsed, and something short and squat flew straight through the dungeon.

One wall collapsed onto the royal executioner. The Jeeves head dropped out of his hands and bounced across the floor, rolling to a stop at my feet.

The flying blur punched a hole straight through the opposite wall and its sensible blue shoes vanished from the room. The wall creaked and moved into the dungeon, first in slow motion and then in a very rapid pile of collapsing brick and mortar. Part of the ceiling came away and crashed in as well. The whooshing sound grew more faint, yet the sounds of banging through distant, falling walls deep inside the palace echoed back to the dungeon, along with a shrill, shouting, robotic voice.

"*We are Albion! We prefer marmalade on our scones and jam on our kippers!*"

The real Queen turned on me, eyes wide with a fear she had never before felt in her life. "What have you done?" she hissed.

"See, here's the thing," I said as I snatched up the Jeeves head like a football and grabbed the old biddy by the arm. *"Run!"*

Chapter 15

We booked it back out through the door just as the Robot Queen made a return visit to the dungeon. The rest of the walls came down and a cloud of thick dust belched out into the hallway behind us.

"Not down here, Mannix," I yelled into the Jeeves robot's decapitated head as we ran. "*I'm* down here, damn it! The upper floors, the *upper* floors!"

"The robot lady is difficult to control, Mr. Crag," the elf's tense voice replied from the speaker at the rear of Jeeves' robotic mouth.

The wall between the dungeon and the hallway came down and the Robo-Queen was suddenly rocketing up the hall behind us.

"*We are Albion! Off with their 'eads!*"

"Up, Mannix, up! Make her go up!"

Back in my office in the States, Mannix must've found the right button on the remote control. The Robot Queen had almost reached us when all of a sudden she swerved up into the ceiling. She punched through and disappeared. I could hear floor after floor giving way as she slammed up higher into the topmost floors of the palace.

There was an elevator at the end of the hallway and, Queen in tow, I jabbed at the lone button. The doors slid open and I dragged the old dame inside. The three princes made it onboard, as well as several advisors, including Hastings.

I made sure the servant with my armload of gardening tools made it on too.

"You are destroying Monmouth Palace!" Hastings cried.

"All part of the plan," I assured them. "First and most important, I want it on the record that anything nice I said back there about one Detective Daniel Jenkins was all a lie as part of the act. Any cop who lets an elf sneak into a hospital room he's supposed to be guarding so that said elf can make a rubber impression of a patient that can be used to make a mask for a robot duplicate isn't fit to write parking tickets at the local public golf course."

The car suddenly lurched and the elevator lights momentarily dimmed. Everybody else grabbed for the railing, but I grabbed the Queen to make sure the old bat didn't fall down and break her crown. I didn't do it to be gallant. Chivalry was dead, but if the Queen cashed in her chips at that moment I'd be out a bundle as well as subject to the final, fatal condition of the Cursed Ruby of Goddamn Pimlico.

The doors dinged open on the first floor of the palace. I got the Queen out safely, and the three idiot princes made it on their own, as well as a couple of advisors. Hastings was last aboard, and he was just getting off when there was a crash from somewhere upstairs. The Robot Queen must've zapped the cable on one of the upper floors, because the car abruptly dropped from sight, trailed down the shaft by falling brick and wood.

The ensuing crash launched dust up the shaft and out the door into the first floor.

Hastings had dropped his satchel just outside the elevator. I grabbed it from the floor and shoved it into the Queen's arms. "You'll be needing this," I assured her.

Our small company wended its way through the downstairs rooms and halls to the back of the palace. We joined a ton of servants who had already fled the building.

By the time we got outside, Monmouth Palace was starting to look like the biggest block of architectural Swiss cheese this side of the Moon Monster's Emmentaler Citadel in the Vallis Alpes. The Robot Queen crashed through a top story window, flew in an arc and headed straight back inside, this time through a wall. One of the chimneys jutting up from the roof shivered and began shedding bricks before collapsing completely. I could see it falling in chunks inside the building through one of the holes the Robo-Queen had blown through the side wall.

"Your terms," the Queen said. "Quickly."

I slapped my bill in her hand. "It's all there. Reimbursement in cash, American, for the original four grand. No curses or any other dirty tricks this time. Used robot purchase and refurbishment from Polly Skidmore's Pawn Shop. A fine establishment which you'd better pay off right away for the damage your Robot Queen caused or Polly just might wind up with a copy of the tape. Let's see, cost of the rush job on that rubber Jeeves mask. Airfare, hotel, transportation. Ten cases of celebratory Seagrams. A generous bonus for my elf pal."

"Thank you, Mr. Crag," Mannix's tiny, tinny voice chirped from the speaker.

"Don't mention it, kid."

"What is this for an exterminator?" the Queen demanded.

"Hey, are you going to quibble, or am I going to bring your whole house down?"

"Outrageous highwayman," the Queen complained. But when she broke open Hastings' satchel, despite her partially frozen fingers, she was real speedy writing the check. "There," she snapped. "Now how do you plan to save us?"

I scrutinized the check carefully before I folded it up and tucked it in my wallet. "Easy," I said, glancing around.

The powdered wig kid with my scythes and pitchfork was standing nearby and silent, like the best caddy the PGA had ever seen. The three princes were a few yards away. The oldest prince was sitting happily up in a tree branch, humming, chatting with an empty bird's nest and seemingly oblivious to the destruction of Monmouth Palace going on above his head. The middle prince was picking the pocket of a cabinet minister, while the youngest prince cleverly distracted the minister by making out with him.

For a minute I wondered if I wouldn't be doing a public service for Albion if I packed it in and left them all at the mercy of the unmerciful mob massed out front. In the end, it was a deep and abiding love for my own hide that won out.

"Junior," I said to the stooge in the powdered wig who was holding the gardening tools, "shake Prince Nitwit down out of that tree and give him my nine iron."

Chapter 16

The Albion papers called it "The Battle for Monmouth Palace." Some battle. It took all of five minutes. But the Albion public ate it like a crap sandwich and begged for a plate of dysentery-laced cow's head for dessert.

I missed my calling. I should have gone into public relations. Once the half-assed battle was over, the sidewalks of the capital had to be temporarily cleared of hookers, codpiece vendors and parents selling factory-age child laborers in order to set up newspaper stands to meet the extra demand. Everybody under the gloomy Albion sky wanted to feel like they were there on that glorious day. There were even articles written about how people had clipped other articles and memorialized the royal family's lies on the fridge door, secured in place by brand-new Monmouth Palace magnets. $25 for a set of two at Ye Olde Palace Rip-off Gift Shoppe.

The Queen was right. Deep down, the people of Albion would accept nearly anything, no matter how ludicrous, that gave cover to their precious royals.

I stopped Mannix from trashing the palace and had him bring the Robot Queen down by remote control in some bushes next to the palace. I sank the pitchfork in her back and handed the scythes to the two younger princes. Prince Gormless led the charge while the Queen and I hid and watched.

The three princes chased the Robo-Queen on foot around to the front of Monmouth Palace. Once they got the full attention of the crowd outside the gates, I ordered Mannix to launch her in the air and hit the destruct button. The Robot Queen blew up in a million pieces over the mob with Prince Gormless' pitchfork in her back, the crowd went nuts in a positive way for the palace P.R. flacks, and the three moron princes became instant heroes.

The Queen went on the air five minutes later. Even when I returned home, I couldn't get away from her speech. Mannix was piping a rerun of it into my office on the radio on Doris' desk when I walked through the front door.

"We could not be more proud of our sons, who have saved the monarchy. After the evil Jeeves had imprisoned us in carbonite and substituted a robot in our place, we feared that all was lost. However, our sons have risen to the occasion and saved not only us, but Monmouth Palace, the very seat of the monarchy in our beloved and most cherished Vauxhall, the very heart of Albion. We only hope that the sinister Jeeves is able to return to these shores to stand trial for his heinous crimes, and does not suffer a fatal accident in his hospital room, as I understand American hospital beds can snap like bear traps, American bedpans can become wedged over one's head in a particular manner known to suffocate one, and that patients in American hospitals frequently commit suicide by jumping out their windows in such a way that, while it looks as if they were dragged to the sill and pushed, they clearly were not."

She'd veered off script at the end. Still, none of my business what happened to Jeeves. Somewhere, the pile of sawdust that had been Merlin was smiling down from wizard heaven. Or screaming up from wizard hell. The guy was kind of a backstabbing bastard when it came down to it. Either way, I was out of it.

"If it's not the horse race results, shut it off," I ordered.

Mannix dutifully snapped off the radio and followed me into my own office, where the radiator was clattering a tin can symphony. There was so much steam in the air I half-expected to find a bunch of fat Russians in towels melting on my desk. Instead, there was the book Merlin gave me and the defunct Robot Queen's useless remote control. I picked them both up and dropped them in the empty wastebasket.

"You take care of the dough?" I asked as I hung up my hat and coat.

Not that I didn't trust royalty in general or the Queen of Albion specifically, but I'd flagged down the first donkey cart I found outside the palace and cashed the check at the nearest bank. I wired the money back to the good ol' U.S. of A. before I left Albion.

"Yes, sir," Mannix said. "I took my bonus and put most of the rest in the bank. You still had $487.50 left from the money the man in the pointy hat paid you."

I already knew that the curse had stopped halving the loot Merlin had exchanged for the ruby since the dough in my wallet had stopped shrinking after the Robo-Queen went boom. I'd saved the Albion monarchy. Bully for me.

"Consider that *my* bonus," I said. "I saw the exterminator's truck downstairs. He do this floor yet?"

"No, sir, Mr. Crag. I think he's still at the back of the fish market downstairs."

"Good. Mice will be the least of his problems down there. Vincetti's normal fastidious standards of cleanliness will keep a team of ten men busy spraying down the fresh haddock for cockroaches for the next two hours." I fished in my wallet and gave Mannix the last of the Pimlico Ruby money as well as a few more bills. "Run out to Staples for a couple supplies, will you? We've got a little change of plans."

# # #

I'd made the arrangements with the exterminator before I left for Albion, since I knew that slob Johansen would never do it. I figured if I survived I'd stiff Albion with the bill and if I got killed it wouldn't matter if the local rat-catcher got paid or not.

That was before I knew that the Queen, Jeeves, the Albion Embassy, the Albion government, the Robot Queen and the entire bastard country that propped them all up was directly responsible for my rodent infestation and lost booze.

The exterminator I'd picked was one of those humane outfits that allegedly treated vermin like they were people and, if they were true to form for jokers like that, treated people like vermin. Mannix had returned with the stuff I'd asked him to pick up, mostly collapsible boxes and packing tape, when the guy in the Pied Piper Exterminators jumpsuit strolled into my office with a scowl and fife.

"You got yourself a rodent sitiation in here, too?" he asked.

He started tootling on his fife before I answered, and a minute later the turtleneck- wearing mice started streaming from the baseboards in a trance.

There were a hell of a lot more of the little plague carriers than I thought. They marched in two neat files out the door, into the hallway and onto the elevator.

Mannix and I joined the exterminator musician and his hypnotized rodent audience for the ride down. He seemed suspicious of us, what with all the junk we were schlepping down with us. I'm sure the smug bastard look on my face didn't help.

"What do you do with them?" I asked, trying real hard to pretend I gave a rat's ass about the lie I knew he was about to tell me.

"None of the rodents are harmed," he said out of the corner of his mouth as he continued to blow. It sounded like "Thick as a Brick," but I wasn't sure since the guy was mostly tone deaf. The mice didn't seem to care. They just swayed along with the discordant tune, and when the doors slid open on the ground floor and he danced out into the hallway, the mini-rats trailed him outside.

"You see, I picked you because I have it on good authority that's bullshit," I said as he tootled them into cages in the back of his van. There were already tons of mice already loaded up from the other floors. "I heard from a demon I know that you sell them to Chinese restaurants all over town as egg roll filler, and that whatever's left gets sold as snake food to pet shops throughout the beautiful tri-city area. Of course, this information will remain between us if you give me ten minutes in the back of the van and if you don't mind billing the Albion embassy for whatever losses you incur in your side businesses."

My new exterminator buddy was more than reasonable, despite the murderous look in his eye and the nastiest version of "Flight of the Bumblebee" you ever heard. Ten minutes was more than enough time. When we emerged from the back of the van eight minutes later, the cages were empty and Mannix and I had a couple of very large boxes taped, addressed, and ready to ship. I checked my watch.

"If you shake a leg, you'll make it to the post office before they close."

"Yes, sir, Mr. Crag." Mannix nodded vigorously and repeated my orders just to make sure. "The first box gets shipped right here in town to the headquarters of the Temperance League. That's where they were all supposed to go originally, right?"

"Right. I'll teach those old bags for trying to turn me into a decent and upright member of society. As for our slight change of plans, the second box goes to Monmouth Palace, care of the wine cellar. I'm just returning to them that which was already theirs before the bastards made theirs mine. Anyway, it's all on the shipping labels."

"Yes, sir, Mr. Crag," the elf said.

"Just don't tell the post office what's in the boxes. Tell them they're Hummel figurines wrapped in newspapers. They've got a thing about mailing vermin overseas. I found that out when I tried to mail Zombie Arafat to France last year."

"Yes, Mr. Crag," Mannix said, nodding. The elf hurried down the sidewalk, teetering beneath the two huge boxes.

"And if there's extra postage, just bill it to Her Royal Ice Cube, Monmouth Palace Ruins, 10 Goat Lane, Vauxhall, Albion!" I hollered down the street.

I turned and headed off in the opposite direction for O'Hale's and a comfortable barstool with my name carved in it. I left it for Mannix to remember the zip code. Hey, I already did too much of everyone else's damn work around here as it was.

ABOUT THE AUTHOR

Jim Mullaney is the ghostwriter, author or co-author of 27 novels, including four books in the New Destroyer series. He has written for Marvel Comics, is co-author of The Destroyer series guide, The Assassin's Handbook 2, and has a short story, Beauty Is As Beauty Dies, in Moonstone's new Green Hornet Casefiles anthology. He is currently working on the third book in Red Menace series.

Jim has a website dedicated to his work and a forum located at http://www.jamesmullaney.com/

He can be reached via email at Housinan@aol.com and he is on Facebook as James Mullaney.

Bonus Preview

One Horse Open Slay

A Crag Banyon Mystery

Dashiell Hammett meets Santa Claus Is Comin' To Town

"Hello, you've reached Banyon Investigations...."

Crag Banyon is just your run-of-the-mill P.I. He's got a secretary who loves to hate and hates to love him. His worst enemy in the world is on the local force and relishes the thought of seeing Banyon behind bars. And he's got a knack for attracting all the crazies to his small downtown office above the fish market. So when an elf shows up on a stolen reindeer and hints of foul play at the North Pole, Banyon takes the whole thing in stride, refuses to take the case, and heads off to his favorite saloon. But when the elf turns up dead the next morning, the cops make their least favorite private eye the fall guy.

A hunted man, Banyon lams it to the Arctic Circle to clear his name. He quickly finds that Santa's workshop is a lot more dangerous than even a plucky P.I. with a ready quip and a five-alarm hangover can handle. Between fighting for his life and fending off the advances of a hot-to-trot Mrs. Claus, Banyon uncovers a conspiracy that goes far past December 25. If he can just ring in the New Year without a bullet in his brain, it'll all be just another day's work for Crag Banyon, P.I.

"....he's an SOB, but he's cheap. How may I direct your call?"

Bonus Preview

Devil May Care

A Crag Banyon Mystery

BANYON'S BACK WITH ONE HECK OF A CASE!

For a savvy private investigator like Crag Banyon, tackling cases that are too hot to handle comes with the territory. But even a plucky P.I. with an occasionally unsavory client roster has his limits. So when a demon shows up at the front door of Banyon Investigations with a pile of cash and a plea for help, Banyon thinks it could be time to cool things down. Unfortunately, temptation strikes at the precise moment the rent is overdue, and the landlord -- not to mention the power and phone companies and Banyon's top fifty favorite liquor stores -- don't take IOUs. Short on cash, he makes a deal with the devil..

Someone's gone over the wall and escaped from Hell, and the demon prison guards need somebody on the outside to track down their misplaced soul. Simple missing persons case, right? Except nothing's ever simple for Crag Banyon, P.I. When he's not being assaulted, mauled, arrested, framed, betrayed, chased and nearly killed, he's uncovering a conspiracy that extends from this life to the afterlife and all points in between.

When all Hell breaks loose, what's Banyon's solution? Shove a flask in his pocket and go to a matinee at the Bijou until it all blows over or blows up...whichever comes first.

Printed in Great Britain
by Amazon